"We've forgotten about room inspection!" Kathryn yelled.

"But the drill's not over!"

"Yes, it is! The lights have stopped flashing!"

Indeed, the Red Alert lights had stopped flashing. Dunkirk cringed. "Oops."

Kathryn started for the lift at a dead run. "Frost, if your daydreaming has made me fail inspection I'll—" She didn't finish but rode the lift back up to the fourth floor and, leaving Dunkirk behind, ran to her room. Other cadets were already back in their rooms, desperately cleaning up for inspection. *So ThrumPol and I weren't the only ones who failed the first time,* Kathryn thought.

"Attention, cadets," came Yeoman Hott's voice over the loudspeaker. "All rooms have failed inspection. Cadets are to report immediately to the Study Lounge on Level One. Repeat, report immediately to the Study Lounge on Level One."

Star Trek: The Next Generation
STARFLEET ACADEMY

#1 Worf's First Adventure
#2 Line of Fire
#3 Survival
#4 Capture the Flag
#5 Atlantis Station
#6 Mystery of the Missing Crew
#7 Secret of the Lizard People
#8 Starfall
#9 Nova Command
#10 Loyalties
#11 Crossfire
#12 Breakaway

Star Trek:
STARFLEET ACADEMY

#1 Crisis on Vulcan
#2 Aftershock
#3 Cadet Kirk

Star Trek: Deep Space Nine

#1 The Star Ghost
#2 Stowaways
#3 Prisoners of Peace
#4 The Pet
#5 Arcade
#6 Field Trip
#7 Gypsy World
#8 Highest Score
#9 Cardassian Imps
#10 Space Camp

Star Trek: Voyager
STARFLEET ACADEMY

#1 Lifeline
#2 The Chance Factor
#3 Quarantine

Star Trek movie tie-ins

Star Trek Generations
Star Trek First Contact

Available from MINSTREL Books

STAR TREK®
VOYAGER™

STARFLEET ACADEMY®

LIFELINE

Bobbi JG Weiss and David Cody Weiss

Interior illustrations by
Jason Palmer

A MINSTREL® BOOK

Published by POCKET BOOKS
New York   London   Toronto   Sydney   Tokyo   Singapore

A MINSTREL PAPERBACK *Original*

A Minstrel Book published by
POCKET BOOKS, a division of Simon & Schuster Inc.
1230 Avenue of the Americas, New York, NY 10020

A VIACOM COMPANY

STAR TREK is a Registered Trademark of Paramount Pictures.

This book is published by Pocket Books, a division of Simon & Schuster Inc., under exclusive license from Paramount Pictures.

ISBN: 0-671-00845-5

First Minstrel Books printing August 1997

10 9 8 7 6 5 4 3 2 1

A MINSTREL BOOK and colophon are registered trademarks of Simon & Schuster Inc.

Cover art by Michael Herring

Printed in the U.S.A.

For George,
"Wasn't that a good idea I had?"
Your SNW

STARFLEET TIMELINE

2264

The launch of Captain James T. Kirk's five-year mission, _U.S.S. Enterprise,_ NCC-1701.

2292

Alliance between the Klingon Empire and the Romulan Star Empire collapses.

2293

Colonel Worf, grandfather of Worf Rozhenko, defends Captain Kirk and Doctor McCoy at their trial for the murder of Klingon chancellor Gorkon.

Khitomer Peace Conference, Klingon Empire/Federation (_Star Trek VI_).

2323

Jean-Luc Picard enters Starfleet Academy's standard four-year program.

2328

The Cardassian Empire annexes the Bajoran homeworld.

2346

Romulan massacre of Klingon outpost on Khitomer.

2351

In orbit around Bajor, the Cardassians construct a space station that they will later abandon.

2353

Kathryn Janeway enters Starfleet Academy.

2355

Kathryn Janeway meets Admiral Paris and begins a lifelong association with the esteemed scientist.

2363

Captain Jean-Luc Picard assumes command of U.S.S. Enterprise, NCC-1701-D

2367

Wesley Crusher enters Starfleet Academy.

An uneasy truce is signed between the Cardassians and the Federation.

Borg attack at Wolf 359; First Officer Lieutenant Commander Benjamin Sisko and his son, Jake, are among the survivors.

U.S.S. Enterprise-D defeats the Borg vessel in orbit around Earth.

2369

Commander Benjamin Sisko assumes command of Deep Space Nine in orbit over Bajor.

2371

U.S.S. Enterprise, NCC-1701-D, destroyed on Veridian III.

Former Enterprise captain James T. Kirk emerges from a temporal nexus, but dies helping Picard save the Veridian system.

U.S.S. Voyager, under the command of Captain Kathryn Janeway, is accidentally transported to the Delta Quadrant. The crew begins a 70-year journey back to Federation space.

2372

The Klingon Empire's attempted invasion of Cardassia Prime results in the dissolution of the Khitomer peace treaty between the Federation and the Klingon Empire.

Source: Star Trek® Chronology / Michael Okuda and Denise Okuda and Star Trek® Voyager™ Mosaic/Jeri Taylor

Chapter

1

Cadet Kathryn Janeway gave her good friend, Anna Mears, a big hug. "You'll be fine," she told Anna, trying to sound optimistic. It wasn't easy, considering her own feelings at the moment.

"Of course I'll be fine," Anna answered. "It's *you* I'm worried about."

"Ah, don't worry about Kathryn." Blake Thomas gave Kathryn's shoulder a confident pat. "She'll have everybody in the dorm playing Parrises Squares up and down the hallways in no time."

"Only because nobody plays a game of good old-fashioned tennis anymore," Kathryn managed to quip. Strange, how her voice sounded so light and happy, nothing like how she felt. She knew Anna and Blake saw through it, though. They'd known her for a long time.

Anna picked up her duffel bag. "Take it easy, both of you. And call me."

"No, you call me," Blake shot back with a grin.

"When you two settle on who should call who first, then call me," said Kathryn. She watched as Blake headed down one path and Anna headed down another. Neither took the path that Kathryn had to take.

Each of those paths led to a different dorm building on the grounds of Starfleet Academy. Kathryn's led her back to the big Administration Building, where she and her two friends had checked in after arriving an hour ago. Then the path wound past a line of sleek, white buildings that housed classrooms, lecture halls, labs, training holosuites and all the other facilities that made Starfleet Academy the exceptional learning institution that it was.

Although the campus was beautifully landscaped, with trees and gardens and acres of thick green grass, Kathryn still felt hemmed in as she walked, as if all these modern, man-made structures were designed to hide the campus from the outside world. Kathryn was used to wide open spaces, the kind she saw every day in rural Indiana. She'd been born and lived all her life there, and she had attended the Academy Institute, an official Starfleet Academy prep school located in Indiana, with Blake and Anna.

And with Cheb Packer, but Kathryn didn't want to

think about Cheb right now. He hadn't been accepted to the Academy like the rest of them, and she was still angry that his jealousy had ruined their relationship.

Kathryn was angry at someone else as well, someone who was supposed to have accompanied her on this trip today instead of Blake and Anna. Someone else was supposed to be with her right now, sharing this, perhaps the greatest moment in her life. But as usual, he was far away. "Business before daughter again, eh, Daddy?" Kathryn muttered, shifting her heavy duffel bag from one shoulder to the other.

Kathryn's father was Vice Admiral Edward Janeway, and for the past few years, ever since the big Cardassian problem began, he'd been off-planet more than on. These days Kathryn spoke to him more via subspace radio than in person. Sometimes she wondered if he knew he even had a family anymore, let alone a daughter who dearly loved and missed him.

Kathryn could forgive all of it, though, if he had just kept one promise—to be with her today. They'd planned this trip all summer. It was going to be perfect. But at the last minute he'd been called away to an urgent conference on Vulcan. All she'd gotten was a subspace message from him: "Sorry, Goldenbird. Duty calls. I'll come visit as soon as I can."

Kathryn's mother had offered to come instead, and so had her oldest and dearest friend, Hobbes Johnson. But she had turned them down. "I don't need anybody to hold my hand," she said to herself as she walked. "If it's too much trouble for my own father to keep a promise, then I'll just do this myself."

Kathryn continued swiftly along the path until Sudak Hall appeared from behind a line of stately oak trees. Despite her mood, she paused a moment. Her heart beat just a little faster at the sight of the tall, sleek building. It might have been a giant magnet, the way new cadets from every direction were heading toward it, their dreams and their luggage in tow. "This is it, Kathryn, your new home sweet home." Steeling herself, Kathryn marched up the steps leading to the big front door. It *whooshed* open and she stepped through.

The dorm's interior was like a travel terminal at rush hour. Beings from a variety of Federation worlds bustled about. Piles of luggage dotted the floor, and everyone seemed to be carrying some kind of duffel, box or bag. The freshmen cadets, not yet in uniform, were easy to distinguish—they were the ones gawking at everything with expressions of awe and excitement. Kathryn tried not to notice how many of them were accompanied by family members who'd come to see them off. Instead she focused on her own expression, fixing a look of fiery confidence on her face as if daring anyone to ask why she was alone.

As Kathryn pressed forward into the crowd, her senses reeled at the rush of variety around her. It was just so much to take in at once, all these different people, the mix of human and alien languages, the swirling colors, the sounds, the smells! Her nose twitched at the spicy scent of a Haliian's perfume, and her hand tingled as an Arbazan's rough cloak brushed against her skin. A serene young Vulcan cadet gestured politely to her, and Kathryn obligingly moved aside to allow his parents to pass by unhindered.

Kathryn crossed the large circular Main Lounge that formed the center of the dorm building. A map of its layout had been included in Kathryn's advanced registration packet, and naturally she had it memorized. She noted that, as the map had shown, all other parts of the dorm could be accessed from the Main Lounge, by stairway or lift: the East Wing of dorm rooms to the left, the soundproofed study halls directly across the lounge, and the West Wing of rooms to the right. The mess hall was up on the second floor.

Kathryn turned to the right. Her room assignment was WW416—West Wing, fourth floor, room 416. She took a lift up four floors and walked down the clean carpeted hallway until she came to room 416.

The door was open. Kathryn heard odd shuffling sounds coming from inside. "Hello?" She had no idea who her roommate would be, but the shuffling noises suggested someone with a large, bulky body. *Please, anything but a Horta,* Kathryn thought, and curiously peeked around the corner. "Hello there? I'm—"

Just as she looked inside, a stack of boxes in the middle of the room toppled. On top of that stack of boxes had been someone of about her own height, who was now crashing down onto someone else also about her height who had been standing next to the stack of boxes. All the boxes and both of the "some-ones" fell to the floor in a noisy jumble.

Kathryn dropped her duffel bag and ran to help. "Are you okay?"

Two identical beings looked up at her. They were humanoid and female, with feathery crests of golden hair that ran from the tops of their heads down their backs. Their bodies were covered in fine golden fur, and they wore matching tunics made of a strange shiny black fabric that shimmered when they moved. As Kathryn stared down at them, she felt as if she were drowning in their enormous golden eyes. . . .

The twins broke out into wide grins, showing perfect little white teeth. "Oh good good good!" one enthused.

"It's a Human!" shrilled the other in excitement.

Quickly they sorted out their tangled limbs and scrambled to their feet, hastily dusting each other off. "We are ThrumPol," they said in unison. "What are you called?"

It took Kathryn a moment to find her voice. The aliens moved so fast, with such precise yet gracefully fluid movements, it was difficult to follow them. "Uh, my name is Kathryn Janeway," she finally managed to say.

The twins reached out and, each grabbing one of her hands, shook them with great enthusiasm until Kathryn feared she'd be jostled off her feet. "We're pleased—"

"—to meet you!"

"We hoped to room with a Human. We've studied your language and—"

"—practiced your hand grabbing greeting, see?"

"Do you prefer a diminutive form of address? Kathy? Kath?"

"Kate? Katie? Kat?"

"Whoa, wait a minute!" Kathryn took a step back, pulling her hands away. "Are *both* of you my roommates?"

ThrumPol nodded in perfect unison. "Is that a—"

"—problem? We thought—"

"—you knew."

"No," said Kathryn, suddenly noticing that there were three beds in the room. "I didn't." Nor should she have known. It was standard practice for roommates to meet upon arrival at the Academy. But Kathryn had never heard of a cadet getting *two* roommates, and she said so.

"There is a good—"

"—reason for this arrangement, Kathryn Janeway." ThrumPol proceeded to explain, each of them finishing the other's sentences and completing each other's gestures until Kathryn felt like she was watching one person who had somehow been split into two.

That's just what the twins were—exact duplicates, like human identical twins. But Thrum and Pol were Diasoman, and everyone on their home world of Diaso II were born twins who lived their young lives together, every minute of every day. As one of them put it, pointing at the other one, "She ate, I belched."

8

ThrumPol explained that Diasoman twins gradually grew apart into separate beings. By adulthood they were full individuals. But the separation process could often be awkward and even frightening for twins who were very close, as were Thrum and Pol. "We're just entering our stage of separation," one of them told Kathryn. "It will be very hard for us—"

"—to lose our link," finished the other, tapping her forehead. Kathryn guessed that the two had some kind of psychic connection. *No wonder they finished each other's sentences,* she thought.

"We're not ready to separate enough to live apart," one confessed.

"So the Academy has allowed us to live together during our freshman year," added the other. "Next year we'll have our own rooms and roommates. But for now—"

"—the Academy has chosen you to share our living quarters."

"So how shall we address you? Kathryn, Kathy, Kate—"

"—Kat, Katrina?"

"Please, just hold on a second!" Kathryn turned away, hoping the hyperactive twins couldn't see her dismay.

The honest truth was that Kathryn didn't want a roommate at all. Classwork was going to be plentiful and difficult, and given the option, Kathryn would have preferred to live alone where she would be free to study whenever and however she wanted. Now she was trapped with *two* roommates about to begin a traumatic life phase. Their nonstop chatter alone would drive her insane before classes even started. Besides all that, Kathryn couldn't even tell which of them was which!

They pointed helpfully at each other. "She is Thrum—"

"—and she is Pol."

Kathryn studied their identical faces, bodies and clothing. "I'm sorry, I can't tell you apart."

"She has larger eyes than I," said one as if it were obvious.

"And she has a bigger nose."

"*Aou!* I do not!"

"Yes, you do!"

"Never mind!" Kathryn broke in. "I'm sure I'll figure it out. Somehow." She walked back to the doorway and picked up her duffel. *I can't deal with this! It's insane!* she thought, but she forced a pleasant smile on her face when she turned back around.

The twins both gestured at the empty bed. "We saved you—"

"—the sleepbed by the window. Is that—"

"—acceptable?"

Kathryn tossed her duffel on the designated bed. It was bare with a set of plain white sheets and a pillow stacked at one end. "Fine. This is great. Thank you." *I'm doomed!* she thought, keeping that smile on her face even as she gritted her teeth in irritation. *I don't have time for this! I want quiet! I*

*want structure! I don't want to room with the dog-
gone Corsican sisters!* Then she sighed. *Kathryn
Janeway, back off. You're angry at Daddy and it's
not fair to take it out on ThrumPol. They can't help
it if they're enthusiastic. At least they're trying to be
nice.* So with effort, Kathryn renewed her smile and
turned back around, only to find the Diasomans
staring at her like kids watching a new puppy, waiting for it to do something amusing.

"We like you," one ventured.

"You have pretty skin," offered the other. "Very
smooth."

"Uhh . . ." Kathryn cleared her throat. "Yes,
well . . . tell me, why were you standing on those
boxes?"

ThrumPol threw each other a guilty glance and immediately went to work restacking the fallen boxes.
One explained, "We were attempting to turn—"

"—the room's lighting device down," finished the
other. "Our eyes are larger than human eyes, and your
light levels—"

"—are too bright for us." One twin tapped her
skull. "Headaches. *Aou!*"

"We ordered lens shields," said the other, indicating
her huge eyes, "but—"

"—they aren't ready yet."

Kathryn tilted her head up slightly. "Computer, dim
lights, please." Instantly the room lights dimmed down
to one-half normal illumination.

ThrumPol looked at Kathryn, at each other, then down at their feet. Even through their fur Kathryn could see their cheeks blush. "I feel—"

"—so stupid."

Kathryn unzipped her duffel and began to unpack, wondering how these two ever passed the Academy's grueling entrance exams. "Don't worry about it. Give yourselves time to adjust to new things. I'm sure Earth is very different from Diaso Two."

Even though her back was turned, Kathryn could hear the twins whisper. "See?" came one quiet voice. "Humans are very understanding."

"Tcht!" the other voiced sharply.

Suddenly a loud rap on the door made them all jump. A short, skinny, out-of-breath cadet waved a hasty greeting, then broke out into a flood of words that whipped by so fast they only barely qualified as Standard Federation English. "Hi-Hally-B.-Coogan-I-live-down-the-hall-got-a-warning-our-CGC-is-Commander-Mallet-he's-on-his-way-so-clean-up-your-room-*now!*" and he was gone.

Kathryn managed to blink once. Then she leaped to the door. "Hey, wait!" But Coogan was already at the door of the next room, delivering his message in the same rapid-fire tones to more fellow freshmen. In seconds he was dashing around the corner, heading for the next room, and his latest informants were yelling, "Hey, wait!" after him, too.

Kathryn turned back to ThrumPol. Their eyes were

narrowed in concentration as they tried to decipher Coogan's word blur. "I didn't understand—"

"—a word he said."

"I did," declared Kathryn. "He said our cadet group commander is Mallet. He must mean Commander Etienne Mallet." She started tidying the room. "We've got to clean up, quick!"

"But—" began Thrum and Pol at the same time.

"Just do it!" ordered Kathryn. Her urgency was contagious, and without another word ThrumPol stacked their boxes and put them into the closet, then quickly started folding clothes and putting them away while Kathryn made her bed so fast the sheets nearly sparked.

Kathryn knew Commander Etienne Mallet. That is, she knew *about* him. He was the Chair of the Sciences Department at the Academy. Of French descent, his name was pronounced "May-lay," and he was brilliant as well as demanding. Being a sciences major, Kathryn had looked up his public Starfleet records, just so she'd know the personality of the man who would, in four years, award her a diploma (with honors, of course) and a shiny new ensign's pip.

But now Fate had thrown Kathryn a nasty curve. Mallet wasn't just her department head, he was her CGC! His records had stated that every few years he took a semester's sabbatical so he could serve CGC duty. Lucky her—*this* was his sabbatical semester.

Kathryn's Academy registration packet had informed her all about the function of a Cadet Group Commander. The theory was this: Along with academic curriculum and physical training, cadets had to be taught to obey orders, act immediately in emergencies, learn drills, and in essence, always be prepared for the unexpected. To this end, each dorm building was thought of as a "starship," and each "starship" was divided into "crews" under the command of a seasoned Starfleet veteran. This veteran, the CGC, lived in the dorm with his or her crew for one semester, performing room inspections and serving as counselor, gadfly, whip, and drillmaster. While juggling classes, homework, physical education and psych training, cadets were also required to perform at any moment for their CGC.

No doubt a very demanding CGC, Kathryn thought as she looked around for a place to stow a very special container that she'd pulled from her duffel.

"What is that?" asked one of the twins, pointing a fuzzy finger at it.

"Coffee beans," Kathryn said. She didn't want to put the beans just anywhere. These were Tarkalian coffee beans, one hundred percent pure and very expensive, a present from dear Hobbes, her friend back home.

"What is coffee?" the other twin asked with curiosity.

"It's a drink that—" Kathryn stopped. Footsteps were coming down the hallway. Mallet! Kathryn was about to make her first impression on a very important man. She stuffed the coffee beans under her pillow, shoved the rest of her unpacked duffel into the closet and tried in vain to straighten her unruly hair. "I'll tell you later," she promised the twins, then jumped as a voice like a pistol shot rang out.

"Attention, cadets!"

Commander Etienne Mallet had arrived.

Chapter

2

He wasn't a tall man, but Commander Etienne Mallet had that same strong, authoritarian bearing that Kathryn's father had when he was in what she called "command mode." *They're about the same age,"* she thought, *and definitely cut from the same mold.* As Mallet stepped through the door, Kathryn snapped to attention. So did ThrumPol.

Mallet's aide was the dorm's watch officer, Yeoman Hott, a young Bolian male with bright blue skin and piercing dark eyes. Like all Bolians, his face was bisected by a horizontal ridge of skin, making him look like he'd been assembled in two pieces from an old-fashioned factory mold. "Room four-one-six, Cadets

ThrumPol and Cadet Janeway," he informed Mallet, reading from a data padd.

"ThrumPol," Mallet said gruffly. "At ease. Now which of you is which?"

"She is Pol, sir," said Thrum.

"And she is Thrum, sir," said Pol.

Mallet stared at them silently for a moment. Then he said, "I remind you, ThrumPol, that all cadets in this institution must distinguish themselves in order to prove their worth to Starfleet. I suggest you two start by simply distinguishing yourselves from each other."

The twins nodded their heads enthusiastically. "We hope to do—"

"—just that, sir!"

Mallet turned to Kathryn. "And Cadet Kathryn Janeway. In the sciences track, as I recall."

"Yes, sir," Kathryn confirmed.

Mallet drew in a slow, deep breath as he studied Kathryn. She fancied he could probably drill a hole through the hull of a starship with his eyes . . . again, just like her father. At that moment she felt as if he were drilling a hole straight into her brain and rummaging around in her memories as if trying to form an instant impression of her whole life. "I expect great things from you, Janeway," he said. It was a command, not a statement of hope.

Kathryn put on her most determined expression. "You'll get them, sir!"

Mallet walked casually around the room. "Now, as you've probably surmised, cadets, this is what's known as a surprise inspection." He brushed at the wrinkles in ThrumPol's bedcovers. "From now on you will keep your room in perfect order at all times. That means no wrinkles in the bedsheets." He made a gesture, and his aide bent down and picked up a gold earring off the floor, which one of the twins accepted with a sheepish grin. "And no rubbish on the floor."

"No, sir!" the Diasomans chorused.

Mallet eyed the suspicious lump under Kathryn's pillow. "And no"—he pulled out the hidden container and read the label—"Tarkalian coffee beans under your pillow." Mallet turned to Kathryn. "I take it you like coffee, Cadet Janeway."

"Uh, yes, sir, I do indeed," she answered cautiously.

"I, too, enjoy a cup now and again," Mallet said. "However, I do not keep beans in my bed."

"Um . . . aye, sir. It won't happen again, sir."

"You're right. It won't." Mallet proceeded to inspect the rest of the room. With the smooth efficiency of a sadistic surgeon, he tore the place apart, piece by piece, moving every item on every shelf, taking everything out of the drawers, checking under the mattresses and, to Kathryn's dismay, opening the closet to find her hastily hidden duffel bag. Worse than saying anything about it, he let a significant pause go by, then simply closed the closet door again.

As far as he was concerned, not one single item was stowed properly. Clothes weren't folded correctly, jewelry was nonregulation, data packs were stacked sloppily, the floor was dirty, the walls had fingerprints,

there was a cobweb in the corner (which there wasn't, Kathryn was sure)—nothing was right. Through it all, Mallet spoke in sharp, quick phrases while Ensign Hott took copious notes on his data padd.

Kathryn didn't move a muscle through the ordeal and neither did ThrumPol. Finally, when the room was a complete mess, Mallet headed for the door. "This room will stand inspection every morning for two weeks," he said.

"Aye, sir!" Kathryn replied, and winced because ThrumPol said the exact same thing at the exact same time. The three of them sounded like a Greek chorus.

One corner of Mallet's mouth quirked up. He left, followed by Hott.

The minute they were gone, Thrum sagged. *"Aou! We are doomed!"*

"Look at our things!" whined Pol. "Does he have the right to do this? And will he do it at every inspection?"

Kathryn didn't answer at first. It took all her concentration not to scream in frustration. *Forget about making a good first impression, Janeway. Mallet's going to remember you as the slob with beans in her bed!* When she was sure her anger was under control, Kathryn hauled her duffel back out of the closet and resumed unpacking. "You two have never heard of boot camp," she said in a clipped voice. "My father told me stories about the armed services on Earth a couple hundred years ago. Back then you couldn't blink without permission. Looks like Mallet is a little old-fashioned."

She eyed the door, thinking of all those stories, of her father, of the fact that he wasn't with her now. Well, wherever he was, he'd be receiving reports of her progress. And no matter how hard she had to work, no matter what she had to do to impress Mallet, those reports were going to make her father proud. "If Commander Etienne Mallet wants perfection, I'll give it to him," Kathryn muttered as she unpacked. "I'll give him more perfection than he knows what to do with!"

Two mornings later, Kathryn awoke early to the soft, silent tingle of the alarm-band around her wrist. She deactivated the device and took it off.

Thrum and Pol were still asleep, each curled like cats in their beds. Thrum was in the bed on the left and Pol was in the bed beyond it. Kathryn grinned. Finally she could tell her roommates apart.

The solution had been deceptively simple—Kathryn merely suggested that one of the twins dye her crest a different color. To her surprise, the Diasomans' responses to that idea demonstrated that they were already beginning to separate, at least in terms of personal taste. Thrum, it turned out, was more conservative than Pol and refused to alter her natural appearance for any reason. Pol, on the other hand, was not only willing to dye her crest, but she decided to dye it shocking violet. Needless to say, nobody had

21

trouble telling the twins apart anymore, including CGC Mallet.

Kathryn slipped on her robe and started to make some coffee, using a little portable grinder-brewer unit designed to operate in perfect silence. She didn't want to wake up the twins, not yet. This wasn't just any morning—this was the first day of classes. Kathryn wanted to start her career off right, with a little peaceful reflection, a fresh cup of java, and one of the homemade caramel brownies that her mother had tucked into her duffel before she'd left home.

Kathryn thought of calling Blake and Anna to wish them good luck today, but she hadn't seen them since they'd all first arrived at the Academy together. Already she and her old childhood friends were drifting apart. Maybe that was to be expected. Kathryn wasn't sure. But it made her feel as if she were shedding an old skin, leaving her feeling itchy and uncertain about the future. Kathryn hated to feel uncertain about anything.

Welcome to the beginning of your life, Kathryn, she thought to herself. What a frightening concept! Was she really up for this? She didn't just want to do good in school—Kathryn wanted to be the best. *If I study hard, I should be able to ace classes,* she thought, *but I'll have to look into extra credit projects and campus organizations to boost my records.* She'd already calculated that she could do with only six, not eight, hours of sleep every night, if she ate right and exercised. Those two extra hours could be used for extra study or volunteer field trips, whatever she needed to keep her name on the top of the lists as the semester unfolded. If she was lucky, she might even find time to join a sports team. That would demonstrate her ability to work with others as well as her physical prowess. *This campus is going to remember me long after I've graduated,* she thought in anticipation. *Daddy will be so proud!*

Kathryn's plotting was interrupted as Pol sat up in bed, her nose twitching as she sniffed the air. "Whuzzat?" she asked sleepily.

"Coffee," answered Kathryn, disappointed that her moment of aromatic peace had been interrupted. "Want some?"

"Is it good?" asked Thrum, opening her eyes and yawning.

Kathryn snorted. "Girls, it is heaven in a cup." She took out three cups and poured some for each of them. She lingered over her first sip as the twins gingerly tasted theirs.

"Aou, numnum!" Pol decided, smacking her lips. Kathryn guessed that *numnum* was a Diasoman word for "yummy." She'd already concluded that *auo* was an exclamation of surprise, like "oh," and *tsht!* meant something like "doggone it!"

Pol glanced over at her sister. "Well? Don't you like coffee, Thrum?"

Wagging her head noncommittally, Thrum said, "It's all right."

Pol squealed in delight, grinning at Kathryn. "Yes!

It's begun, Kathryn! I like something, Thrum does not! We're growing apart!"

"Shhhh!" Kathryn hissed. "You'll wake up the whole dorm!"

Kathryn needn't have worried. A horrendously loud klaxon suddenly went off through the whole building and a voice announced over the loudspeaker, *"Red Alert! Red Alert! All hands to battle stations!"*

Chapter

3

The three cadets froze as the klaxon continued to wail. "I don't believe this!" Kathryn said. "A drill? On the first morning of classes?"

"But we're not dressed!" Thrum yelled over the sound.

Pol poked her twin. "I believe that's the point, *noznit*—it's a surprise!"

The cadets kicked into high gear and their room became a flurry of rushing bodies and scattered clothes. Kathryn put on her uniform in record time, yanked on her boots, slapped on her comm badge, then turned just in time to see Thrum hopping around on her furry left foot, struggling to pull her boot onto her furry right foot. She got it on, but with a grunt of anger yanked it back off. *"Aou!* No socks! Uniform regulations—"

"Forget regulations, this is a Red Alert!" Pol told her, pulling her jumpsuit up over her fuzzy shoulders. "Just get your boots on!"

Thrum started hopping again as Kathryn raced for the door. "I'm going. Hurry up, you two!"

"We are coming!" Pol assured her, about to put on her own boots. Then she frowned at her twin. *"Tsht!* you took my socks!"

"You said you didn't need them," said Thrum smugly. "It's a Red Alert."

Kathryn left as the twins started arguing in Diasoman, a language that sounded like "German spoken underwater by a toothless cat," according to Theda Marr, a cadet who lived down the hall. Kathryn was amazed that such a bizarre description could be so accurate.

The hallway was filled with cadets all scrambling to get to their stations, which Mallet had assigned the previous day. Just like on a real starship during a real emergency, Kathryn and her peers had to get to their stations and perform duties no matter what they'd been doing before, no matter how they felt, and no matter what might happen during the drill.

Dorm drills were designed to catch the cadets by surprise at unusual times, thus training them in a way that a scheduled, programmed holodeck test couldn't. *Well, I'm surprised, all right!* Kathryn thought as she ran down the hall. *The problem is I* shouldn't *be. I should have* known *Mallet would throw something like this at us on the first day of classes.* Mallet's appraisal of their performance during these drills counted as much as their class grades did. *Kathryn Janeway, don't you dare blow it this early in the game!*

She slipped inside the lift just before the doors shut. As it began a swift descent, she noticed that Hally Coogan was standing next to her. He stuck out like a sore thumb from the rest of the cadets crowded in the little cubicle, including Kathryn herself. While they all looked as if they'd dressed during a hurricane, Coogan's uniform was crisp and his hair was neatly combed. Even his boots were polished. It was as if he'd been expecting this drill. "Geez, Coog, did you even go to bed last night?" said a tall blond cadet with the wildest case of bed-head Kathryn had ever seen. She absently ran her fingers through her own hair. It was a hopeless gesture. Without a thorough combing, her hair stuck out all over the place. If only she'd thought to grab a hair clip, at least!

Coogan just looked superior. "Obviously, I'm faster than you greenhorns," he said.

"Hey, who are you calling a—" Kathryn began, but then the lift doors *whooshed* open and the cadets piled out.

"Okay, floor two, Station Thirteen," Kathryn said to herself, turning to the right.

"Hey, that's my station, too!" said the bed-headed blond. "Let's go!"

The klaxon continued its earsplitting wail as they raced down the hallway, dodging other cadets who were scrambling to their stations. They quickly found Station 13, a mock sensor processing console in an alcove.

None of the drill stations were real. They were only training consoles hooked into a central computer that controlled the details of the drill scenario. Among the other stations scattered throughout the dorm building, was a mock console on the first floor that was programmed to operate like a weapons console, a mock warp core assembly down in the basement with several engineering stations for engineering majors, and a mock bridge up on the top floor where several command track cadets had been assigned. In many ways the dorm building really was a starship.

When Bed-head reached Station 13, he immediately began to run a required status check. Kathryn grabbed him by the shoulders and physically joggled him over to the other side of the console. "This is post Thirteen A. You're Thirteen B, over there."

"Oh, sorry." Bed-head shrugged and started running the status check on his side of the console.

"Stats check is my job," Kathryn told him sharply. "You're supposed to monitor the incoming aft array sensor readings."

"Oh, right. Sorry again!" Bed-head grinned. "First day jitters. Don't worry, I'm not usually an idiot." He paused, then added, "I don't *think*."

Under other circumstances Kathryn might have

laughed at that. But this wasn't the time for chitchat. "Readings indicate we've encountered an ion storm. Shields are holding. Sensor data is coming in clear from the forward arrays."

"And clear as crystal from the aft arrays," said Bed-head. "Now all we have to do is make sure the bridge gets all this data." The wailing klaxons suddenly stopped. Only the bright Red Alert light panels continued to flash. Bed-head relaxed a little. "We've gone down to Yellow Alert. Thank goodness. My ears are killing me."

Kathryn was only partially listening to him. Standing down from a Red Alert might make other cadets relax, but as far as she was concerned the emergency wasn't over yet. Station 13 was responsible for making sure all sensor data reached the bridge, and she'd do her job until the drill was officially over. Kathryn Janeway intended to get perfect marks at the Academy, and the time to start that record was now.

"By the way, my name's Dunkirk Frost." Bed-head held out his hand for a shake. "What's yours?"

Kathryn ignored Dunkirk's proffered hand and kept her eyes glued to her sensor readout screen. "Kathryn Janeway. Data is still transferring smoothly."

Dunkirk lowered his hand. "Look, this is an easy post, Kathryn. The second Mallet assigned me here, I read up on this system, tech specs and all. Heck, I could probably build one of these things now. You don't need to sweat so hard, we're in the clear."

Kathryn glanced up at him, for the first time noticing that he was a pretty handsome guy. That is, he would be once his hair was combed. Automatically she ran her fingers through her own hair, wishing that it wasn't so unruly. She hated her hair. Dunkirk watched, looking amused. "What's so funny, Frost?" Kathryn asked suspiciously.

His eyebrows rose high on his forehead. "Me? Nothing. It's just that this is our first day, you know? I can't believe I'm really here, at Starfleet Academy, finishing up my very first drill." He shuffled his feet, looking embarrassed. "It's just exciting, that's all. I've wanted this for so long."

"Me, too." Kathryn returned her gaze to the console readouts. "Too bad it isn't real."

"Hey, it's close enough," said Dunkirk. "We have to learn the ropes, right? But soon we'll be doing this on a real starship somewhere up there." He tilted his head back and stared at the ceiling as if he could see the stars far beyond. "I've never been in space before."

That was a statement one didn't hear from an Academy cadet very often. "You're joking," Kathryn said.

"Nope. My folks are scared of space travel. They've never been off Earth. They don't believe man belongs among the stars." He shook his head in amazement. "As you might guess, they aren't so keen on my being here. When I learned I passed the entrance exams, I tried to book a quick trip on the Luna shuttle, just so I could say I'd been off-planet at least once. My folks canceled it. I didn't push them." He looked up again. "I'll get there soon enough."

Kathryn realized how privileged she was to have a father already in Starfleet. She'd always felt an uncanny connection to the stars. Her father had called her his little "Goldenbird" ever since she could remember. She'd hardly learned to walk when he'd taken her aboard the Luna shuttle, and when she was only nine years old he'd taken her along on a business trip to the Mars Colony. She'd even been allowed onto a starship once, a Miranda-class vessel, to bid her father farewell before he left for an important conference on Deep Space Four. She could still remember the low hum of the warp engines far beneath her feet, a soft rumble like the breath of a great sleeping dragon.

Dunkirk Frost must have worked hard to gain acceptance to the Academy without experiences like that to feed his dreams. With his kind of drive, he'd go places in Starfleet. Kathryn found herself wishing him luck. And then she gasped. "Oh no!"

Her cry startled Dunkirk. "What?"

"We've forgotten about room inspection!"

"But the drill's not over!"

"Yes, it is! The lights have stopped flashing!"

Indeed, the Red Alert lights had stopped flashing. Dunkirk cringed. "Oops."

Kathryn started for the lift at a dead run. "Frost, if your daydreaming has made me fail inspection I'll—" She didn't finish but rode the lift back up to the fourth floor and, leaving Dunkirk behind, ran to her room. Other cadets were already back in their rooms, desperately cleaning up for inspection. *So ThumPol and I weren't the only ones who failed the first time,* Kathryn thought.

The Diasoman twins growled at her in unison when she entered. Kathryn didn't take it personally—she'd already learned that they growled when they were annoyed. *Now's a good time to be annoyed,* she thought. She wished she could growl as well as they could.

"Attention, cadets," came Yeoman Hott's voice over the loudspeaker. "All rooms have failed inspection. Cadets are to report immediately to the Study Lounge on Level One. Repeat, report immediately to the Study Lounge on Level One."

"What?" Kathryn cried. "We haven't even gotten inspected yet! How could we have failed?"

Thrum muttered, "I wouldn't be surprised if Mallet came by—"

"—while we were at our drill posts," finished Pol, her big golden eyes narrowed to angry slits.

Kathryn just grabbed a hair clip from her dresser, jammed her unruly locks through it and marched back to the lift, followed by ThrumPol.

When they reached the Study Lounge, Mallet was there waiting. Hott stood with him as the rest of the cadets under Mallet's command filed in, about two hundred in all. Kathryn caught sight of Dunkirk as he entered and was glad that he kept his distance. She blamed him for this, although deep inside she knew

that she'd been daydreaming at her post as much as he had.

When all cadets were present, Hott gestured for silence. The room grew quiet. "I'm sure you're all pleased to hear that no one was singled out for daily room inspection," Mallet boomed. "You've *all* failed this morning and I'll tell you why. I've been at this game for a long time. I know what cadet rooms look like after the first surprise drill. I don't need to see them."

"Then what's the point?" Kathryn grumbled under her breath. "It wasn't fair!"

Mallet's eyes swept over the assembly. They zeroed right in on Kathryn. "Hard Lesson Number One, Cadet Janeway," he said in a pleasant tone. *"Unfair* is not a Starfleet concept. Life is unfair. Death is unfair. Space is unfair. Deal with it."

Kathryn almost fainted. *He heard me,* she thought in a panic. *Oh my gosh, he heard me! But that's impossible! How could he have heard me? He's way over there and I'm way over here!* Her mind ran frantic little circles around itself and the wild pounding of her heart blotted out everything Mallet said next. Physically Kathryn didn't move a muscle, but in her head, the universe was imploding.

It seemed as if whole years passed before the room around her came back into focus and Mallet's voice became intelligible again. "There's a little something you freshmen need to know," he was saying. "I'll keep it simple. We don't want you here."

Kathryn heard Pol start to growl, but the Diasoman abruptly stopped for fear of being overheard.

"It's up to *you* to convince us that we *do* want you," Mallet continued. "Your entrance exam only gave you the opportunity to come here. Now you have to prove to us that you're worth keeping. If it were up to me, I'd flunk the lot of you now and save Starfleet the time and expense of washing you out one by one.

"You see, as a member of Starfleet, not only will the fate of your fellow shipmates and those under your command hang on your slightest actions, but upon occasion entire civilizations, planets, even whole star systems, will live or die by your performance. We don't want *competent* beings. That's a given. What we expect is the impossible as a matter of daily duty. If you don't think you're up to that, leave now."

On cue, Yeoman Hott stepped to the door, causing it to *whoosh* open. He held it open. Mallet said nothing. Nobody moved.

"There are plenty of civilian careers out there. Many of you have sufficient training to start now," Mallet said. Still nobody moved. Yeoman Hott let the door *whoosh* closed.

"So, you all think you can make it here. Well, it's my job to prove you wrong." CGC Mallet paused dramatically. "That will be all, cadets. Dismissed!"

The assembly dispersed in an orderly fashion until someone said, "Whoa, I'm late for class!" As if the floor had suddenly become electrified, all the cadets broke into a run, surging toward the exit like a living tsunami.

Kathryn hung back. She studied Mallet as he watched the stampede with a stoic expression. Somehow she knew he was amused. *Well, you're not going to get any more amusement out of me!* she thought. With calm, measured steps, Kathryn headed for the door, her head held high, her posture perfect. She was the last one out of the room.

She could feel Mallet's stare as she made her grand exit alone.

Chapter

4

A week later, Kathryn was alone again. But this time, she wasn't at the end of a line, she was at the very front.

She stood before the food replicator in the mess hall, her hands on her hips, a scowl on her face. "Okay, let's try it one more time." She was losing patience, and so were the dozen or more cadets lined up behind her. Kathryn didn't care. The replicator was going to get her order right if she had to gut the thing and reprogram it herself. "I want a salad," she said, "but put in raspberry flavored gelatin cubes with little marshmallows in them."

The replicator made its pleasant *whirring* noise, and

a bowl appeared. Like the four bowls before it, it contained greens, some vegetables, oil-and-vinegar dressing and no gelatin cubes. "Computer, you're supposed to be able to make substitutions!" Kathryn snapped, shoving the bowl back in to be recycled.

The computer's smooth voice replied, "The Oxford English Dictionary, year 2340, defines salad as being 'a cold dish of herbs or vegetables usually uncooked and chopped up or sliced, to which is often added hard-boiled egg, cold meat, fish, etc., the whole being seasoned with salt, pepper, oil and vinegar.'"

Kathryn gritted her teeth so hard her jaws ached. This first week at the Academy was turning out to be frustrating enough, and now she couldn't get a simple salad like her mother used to make.

"Hey, are you about finished up there?" came an exasperated voice near the back of the line.

Kathryn whirled around, her temper flaring. "When this excuse for a junkpile gives me what I want," she said, "I'll be finished, got it?"

The other cadets raised their eyebrows at her outburst, and Kathryn quickly turned back to the replicator, her cheeks burning. *When are you ever going to learn to watch your mouth?* she admonished herself. *What if an upperclassman had walked by and heard you?* She knew she should just take the dictionary salad and let the others have their turn. But when Kathryn Janeway set her mind on a thing, a herd of wild targs couldn't stop her. She focused her glare back on the replicator. "This is your last chance, machine. I want a bowl with chopped lettuce, chopped endive, chopped celery, cucumber, green onion, radish, carrot, *and little cubes of raspberry gelatin with little marshmallows in them.*"

The replicator *whirred.* A bowl materialized. Just as Kathryn reached for it she heard a familiar laugh. She whirled around to see a young, handsome cadet strolling through the mess hall. Her heart skipped a beat. What was her old boyfriend doing here, and in a cadet uniform? *"Cheb?"* she choked.

She almost dropped her bowl. Fortunately the cadet behind her yelled, "Watch it!" and she fumbled a bit but regained her grip. When she looked up again, the young cadet was waving at somebody in line behind her.

"Hey, Riker, did you ace the anthropology quiz?" asked the person in line.

"Darned right I did!" Riker answered, and with a beaming smile, he exited the mess hall.

Kathryn stared after him, even as her brain insisted, *That wasn't Cheb, Kathryn. That Riker guy looks just like him, but it wasn't Cheb.* She shook her head as if to shake away old memories, and in a daze, took her bowl and fork and quickly left the line, oblivious to the sarcastic applause of the cadets behind her.

As she hunted around for a vacant table, Kathryn resolved to avoid Cadet Riker. Her heart was still pounding and a complicated knot of dark emotions roiled around in her chest, creating a sensation that bordered on physical pain. Obviously she hadn't gotten over her breakup with Cheb Packer last summer after all. *He rejected you,* she reminded herself firmly, *simply because you got into Starfleet Academy and he didn't. This is just one more example of the necessity of the Prime Directive.*

Kathryn wasn't referring to Starfleet's Prime Directive, the rule that prohibited Starfleet personnel from interfering with the development of alien cultures. No, Kathryn Janeway had formulated her own personal Prime Directive: "There will be no emotional attachments at Starfleet Academy." The last thing she needed was to fall for Riker, or someone like him, and get her heart stuffed through the meat grinder of romance all over again. It just wasn't worth it.

In fact, Kathryn had decided to keep her distance from everybody. There simply wasn't enough time in a day to do all the things she had to do for school, let alone be social on top of it all. In order for her to be the best, something had to be sacrificed along the way. So be it. She'd never been very social anyway.

Kathryn chose an empty table and sat down. Only when she poked her fork into her salad bowl did she finally notice the contents: greens, vegetables, oil-and-vinegar dressing and no gelatin cubes. "Oh, never mind!" She stuffed the forkful into her mouth and started chewing.

Formulating the Prime Directive had been a brilliant move, but getting the idea across to her peers hadn't been easy so far. *How do the others find so much time to play?* she wondered. It seemed as if

ThrumPol were taking part in every activity on campus, and they kept trying to drag Kathryn along with them. Kathryn's classmates kept trying to draw her into study groups, even after she told them that she preferred to study alone. Even Bed-head Frost had invited her out to a holopic the night before, but she'd turned him down. Nicely, of course, but still, she wondered how on earth he had time to even *think* about holopics with all the homework to be done.

Kathryn finished her lunch and hurried to physical training class. Unlike some people, she liked to eat a light meal before exercising. By the time she'd suited up in her padded exercise sweats and gently stretched out her muscles, her stomach was safely empty again and a boost of energy coursed through her body. She jogged over to the starting line where the rest of the cadets in the class were gathering, among them ThrumPol.

"Everyone ready?" called their coach, Lieutenant Henry Lietas. He was so young and baby-faced that many cadets made the mistake of thinking he was easygoing. Lietas was anything but that. "Remember, cadets, this obstacle course is for conditioning and stamina only. Pace yourselves. It's an exercise, not a race." He held up an old-fashioned starter's pistol and, at the sound of its sharp *crack,* the line broke.

Kathryn leaped forward and took the lead. Remembering Lietas's words, she didn't go too fast, but she still wanted to be first.

ThrumPol jogged up to her, looking like twin teddy

bears in their padded sweats with their furry arms and legs sticking out. "Kathryn!" said Thrum. "Where were you—"

"—this morning?" finished Pol.

Kathryn grimaced as she jogged along, suddenly remembering that the twins had invited her to a breakfast meeting of some campus group they'd joined. In her haste to finish studying for an astrophysics quiz, she'd completely forgotten about it. "I'm sorry, ThrumPol, I couldn't make it. I had to study."

"You said that last night—"

"—when Dunkirk invited you to the holopic."

Kathryn managed to shrug as she jogged. "I study a lot," she said, and with that, she dived into the first obstacle on the course, a metal tube twelve meters long. The hot afternoon sun had heated the tube's surface, and as she crawled along, Kathryn's hands and knees grew warm, even through their protective padding. She crawled faster. The moment she emerged out the other end, Thrum and Pol emerged from their tubes as well.

Thrum threw Kathryn a critical glance as all three of them began the short jog to the next obstacle, a towering wall they had to climb. "But you never stop studying," noted Thrum. "Doesn't your brain—"

"—hurt after a while?" picked up Pol.

"Never!" said Kathryn, and she grabbed one of the ropes dangling from the top of the wall and used it to help her climb. The exertion of her muscles and the purely physical level of her concentration blotted out

ThrumPol's last comment. All Kathryn wanted to do was get through this obstacle course as fast as possible. Anything else was immaterial at the moment.

She reached the top of the wall, followed closely by ThrumPol. All three girls heaved themselves over to the other side and, again using the ropes, slid swiftly back down to the ground. They picked up jogging again, heading for the next obstacle, a double line of big plastic rings lying flat on the ground. They were supposed to hop through the rings on one foot at a time. According to the stories Kathryn's father had told her about twentieth century boot camp, this exercise used to be done using old rubber automobile tires.

"Since you missed our breakfast," Pol began, "would you like to—"

"—join us for dinner?" Thrum finished as they all started hopping through the rings.

"Thanks," Kathryn replied, "but I'm probably going to eat at my desk. I have to finish an exobiology paper."

They finished hopping through the rings and resumed jogging, but now the twins looked upset as well as winded. "Don't you like us?" they chorused.

A little Red Alert klaxon went off in Kathryn's head. "No, that's not it at all," she hastily assured the twins. "I like both of you very much."

"Then why do you reject us?" asked Thrum.

It was becoming difficult to talk this much and exercise at the same time, but Kathryn knew she had to explain herself before her roommates got the wrong impression. "I'm not rejecting you, ThrumPol. It's just that some humans, like me, are unusually ambitious. I want a career in Starfleet more than I've ever wanted anything in my life. I've wanted it since I was a little girl. I don't want to blow it, that's all."

"Blow it?" Pol asked in confusion.

"Mess it up," explained Kathryn. "Ruin my chances."

"Oh!" Pol giggled at Thrum. "What a wonderful idiom! Blow it!"

"So that's why I don't socialize much," Katherine concluded. "I have too much to do."

"But other human cadets are quite festive," Thrum pointed out. "Why are—"

"—you different?" finished Pol.

The question startled Kathryn. *Are you so different?* she asked herself. Before she could formulate an answer, Dunkirk appeared at her side. He looked out of place, dressed in his full cadet uniform and carrying a load of data packs in his arms. He grinned at Kathryn, keeping pace with her and ThrumPol. "Hi! Sorry to interrupt like this, but I was in the area and—"

Pol's giggling interrupted him. "Dunkirk, you are so odd!"

"Not at all," Dunkirk said cheerily as he jogged along, fumbling with the data packs. "I just wanted to catch superwoman here and see if she wanted to come to a concert with me this Saturday night." Catching Kathryn's eye, he added, "The San Francisco Symphony Orchestra is playing on campus. I understand you like Mozart."

The little klaxon in Kathryn's head blared its warning louder. "Dunkirk, I can't," she said, even though he was right—she loved the music of Mozart.

"Aw, c'mon, Kathryn," pressed Dunkirk. "You've got to have some fun sometime, don't you?"

Before she realized that she'd done it, Kathryn stopped jogging. ThrumPol and Dunkirk kept going a few feet, then also stopped. They looked back at her quizzically. "Okay, look," Kathryn began as a strange sense of panic welled up inside of her. "You guys are being sweet, really you are. But classes come first. That's why we're here, isn't it? None of us have time to waste playing around, right?" Lamely she added to Dunkirk, "Thanks anyway, Frost."

Kathryn's panic melted into guilt as Dunkirk blinked at her, looking very disappointed. "Okay," he said in a small voice and walked away.

ThrumPol glanced at Dunkirk, then back at Kathryn. Before they could say anything, Kathryn threw them a cheery smile and said hopefully, "Okay, girls, let's put on some speed!" Ignoring Lietas's instructions, Kathryn took off again, passing all the cadets who had leisurely caught up with her while she'd been standing there. She focused her mind entirely on the strain of her legs and lungs and tried desperately to ignore the sting in her heart.

She wasn't surprised when ThrumPol didn't follow.

Chapter

5

That evening, Kathryn walked briskly across campus, a small program chip clutched in her hand and a mental argument going full blast in her head. *You should be able to handle this on your own,* the rational part of her kept saying. *You don't need to do this.*

The emotional part of her disagreed. *You just want to visit her, that's all,* it argued. *If you hadn't planned on ever visiting her, you wouldn't have brought her along in the first place, right?*

That seemed to settle the argument, at least for now. Kathryn hurried down the path, past the Admin Building, past the fountain and onto the campus Holo Center. There cadets could use holosuite facilities on their personal time for personal matters. The Center offered a variety of simulations for academic extra credit, relaxation, sports activities requiring non-Earth environments, plus thousands more programs, some educational, some strictly for entertainment.

Kathryn had booked a holosuite for one hour, but she didn't need to rent a program. Upon entering the small, empty room, she inserted the program chip she'd been carrying into the control panel. She didn't notice that her hands were shaking and her heart was beating just a little too fast. She merely told the computer, "Run program."

Instantly the room changed. Its black-and-yellow gridded walls shimmered, disappeared, and Kathryn suddenly found herself standing in a huge open field with a blue sky overhead and firm earth under her feet. In fact, the earth under her feet was more than firm—it was oiled and pressed dirt.

Kathryn breathed in deeply, savoring the clean country air. A low buzzing noise started up behind her and she smiled, looking over her shoulder to see a small black dot in the sky. As it approached, the buzzing turned into the rumble of a primitive combustion engine. The dot became an old biplane flying straight at her!

Kathryn ducked and the biplane flew past barely fifteen feet over her head. Its wheels touched down on the dirt-packed runway, and it rolled to a stop next to several other planes parked outside an enormous hangar.

Kathryn straightened back up, grinning harder than ever. She loved this holo-stimulation. It had taken her weeks to research and program this 1930s rural airstrip, the kind that had dotted the open fields of Middle America back when mankind had first taken to the skies. This was the kind of airfield that had been used by one of Earth's first female pilots, Amelia Earhart.

"Well, look who the cat dragged in. It's Katie Janeway!" Amelia herself leaped out of the biplane and waved. She was a petite woman dressed in baggy, grease-smeared coveralls. Pulling off her tight leather aviator's cap, she ruffled her fingers through her brown hair until it fluffed back out into a practical cropped cut, not very stylish, but Amelia wasn't one to worry about fashion. She was an aviator, the first woman to fly solo across the Atlantic Ocean.

She was Kathryn Janeway's hero.

Kathryn jogged up to greet her holo-friend, putting out a hand for a cordial handshake. Amelia frowned. "What'sa matter, you already been at the Academy so long you forgot how to greet an old friend?" With that, she pulled Kathryn into a tight bear hug.

"I forgot how strong you are!" Kathryn grunted.

"I'm only as strong as you programmed me to be," Amelia replied, and she maneuvered Kathryn back an arm's length so she could take a good look at her. "Nice uniform, kid. Except for the grease, maybe."

Kathryn looked down at herself. "You got it all over me!"

"Ah, it'll come out." Amelia chuckled. "Besides, now you'll fit in around here. C'mon, I'll get you a soda pop and we can talk. I take it you didn't come here for flying lessons."

Kathryn followed Amelia into the hangar, a big domed structure that could house as many as six two-seater planes at once. Four were there now, in various states of disassembly as mechanics poked and prodded with archaic tools that Kathryn usually saw only in history texts. Engine parts, more tools and piles of filthy rags littered the floor. The place smelled of machine oil.

"Hope you don't mind talking while I work on the *Dust Devil* over there," Amelia said. "Engine needs a tune-up. Here." She grabbed up a bottle of soda from a box in the corner and handed it to Kathryn. True to the holo-program's 1930s parameters, the soda was room temperature. "Sorry, kid, no ice. Refrigerators won't be common appliances for another twenty years, after all."

Kathryn laughed. She was used to Amelia's wry observations of the differences between her 1930s holo-world and Kathryn's twenty-fourth-century reality. Unlike most holosuite characters, Amelia was self-aware.

Years ago, Kathryn's teachers at the Meadows Elementary School back in Indiana had worried that she was too competitive for her age. When Kathryn refused to discuss the idea, dismissing it as ridiculous, the school counselor assigned her a holocounselor with the hope that she might open up to an imaginary person if not a real one. What he didn't expect was that Kathryn would modify the program to suit *her* imagination.

After much research, Kathryn reprogrammed the original office environment into a 1930s airstrip and reprogrammed the counselor to look and sound like her hero, Amelia Earhart. Kathryn had based Amelia's looks and voice on historical fact, but Amelia's personality was Kathryn's creation.

Despite her new personality, Amelia still functioned as a counselor. She could access informational databases to support her advice, but she never judged or reprimanded Kathryn. She just listened. Over the years, Amelia became Kathryn's best friend, her lifeline throughout childhood and the one person Kathryn could always rely on after her father's work took him away. For all those yeas, no one knew of Amelia's existence. Kathryn kept it a secret. It was a secret still.

"So," Amelia said, examining the *Dust Devil's* engine, "what's on your mind, kid?"

Kathryn shrugged. "I just wanted to visit. I haven't seen you for a while."

Amelia laughed. "It's not like I'm hard to find." Using a pair of pliers, she gripped something deep in the engine and tugged. "So let's see, you've been at Starfleet Academy for, what, two weeks now?" Amelia was accessing Kathryn's public computer files for pertinent data even as she spoke. "You're doing swell in academics, surprise surprise. You're smarter than I ever was, that's for sure. Making friends?"

Kathryn watched Amelia work, fascinated by the antique engine. "I guess."

"Is that a yes or a no?"

Kathryn laughed. "A yes. I guess." Her laugh faded. All humor seemed to drain from her, leaving an emptiness that was almost physically painful. "I don't know . . . I feel . . ." Kathryn tried to continue, but her voice failed. She always had trouble talking about her feelings, even to Amelia. Now she couldn't even make a sound. Words simply refused to leave her mouth. She blinked rapidly, surprised at the tears forming behind her eyes

Amelia pretended not to notice and continued to tinker with the *Dust Devil's* engine. "Look, Katie, you've always had trouble fitting in. Comes from being a perfectionist. Now it's even harder because you're in a place where you can't make the rules." She glanced at Kathryn. "And boy, do I know how you like to run the show."

"That's not true!" said Kathryn. "I don't want to run anything, I just want to . . . I don't know." She sighed with frustration. "There's nobody I can talk to, that's all."

"What, your Universal Translator ain't working?"

"Oh, very funny!"

"You're getting mad. We must be touching on something important." Amelia stopped working and leaned close. "Who're you mad at, kid?"

Kathryn opened her mouth, but like an elusive butterfly, her voice escaped her again.

"Me?"

Kathryn shook her head.

"A teacher?"

Another shake.

"Your roommates?"

Kathryn thought of ThrumPol. They weren't always easy to deal with, but they weren't the problem. Not all of it, anyway. "So much is going on, Amelia, I feel like I'm running all the time, but I don't know where I'm going anymore. I should be able to handle this, but I just . . ." She bit her lip, unable to say the last word.

"Can't?" Amelia suggested bluntly.

"I *can!*" Kathryn cried out. "I *have* to!"

"Kid, why don't you talk to a counselor—"

"I can't talk to an Academy counselor," Kathryn said angrily. "Anything I say will go on my permanent record, you know that. I don't want to worry Mom, and I certainly can't talk to Phoebe." Kathryn shook her head, wondering about her younger sister. "She doesn't understand anything."

"What about your father?" Amelia asked softly.

Kathryn snorted. "What *about* him?"

"I asked you first."

Kathryn scowled. Edward Janeway understood his little "Goldenbird" better than anyone. He always knew how to help Kathryn put her problems into perspective. But when she'd called home yesterday her father wasn't home. He had returned from the conference on Vulcan only to be whisked away again, this time to a meeting on some starbase or another. "He doesn't have the time," she said flatly.

Amelia set her pair of pliers on the edge of the engine case and stared Kathryn right in the eye. "You're very close to your father, Katie. I know how you drive yourself to perfection just to please him. But the fact is, life isn't you-and-Dad-against-the-world anymore. You're grown up now, and you've got duties here, just as he's got duties out there. His work on the Cardassian problem will have an impact on the future politics of the whole galaxy. Kid, instead of being mad at him, why don't you try to be proud of him?"

Kathryn's jaws clenched. Before she could stop herself, she threw her bottle of soda pop against the wall, where it smashed, splattering warm fizz everywhere. "I'll be proud of him when he's proud of me!" she yelled. "And I'll never know whether he's proud of me or not if he never *talks* to me anymore!"

With that, Kathryn ran out of the hangar. The bright sunshine blinded her for a moment, but she kept on running, following the runway across the open field. Deep inside she wanted to hear Amelia call her back, but she knew Amelia's programming was too smart for that. If Kathryn wanted to leave, Amelia would let her leave, knowing that Kathryn would come back when she was ready.

When she'd finally run far enough that her exhaustion outweighed her anger, Kathryn stopped, panting. "Computer, end program." Instantly the open field, the sunshine and the distant hangar disappeared and was replaced by the holosuite's black-and-yellow gridded walls. Like the holo-grease stain on Kathryn's uniform, Amelia Earhart and her world were gone.

Taking her program chip from the computer control panel, Kathryn left the holosuite, growling in sheer frustration almost as well as ThrumPol.

Chapter

6

"Red Alert! Red Alert! Port sections to battle stations! Repeat, port sections to battle stations!"

Kathryn was up and out of bed before she was even awake. She and ThrumPol stood in the middle of their dark dorm room in their pajamas, trying to figure out what was happening. "It's a drill!" Thrum suddenly cried.

"No kidding!" said Kathryn, awake now. "Port stations only. Pol, that's you and me. Let's go!" Kathryn and Pol hurried into their uniforms as Thrum scrambled back to her bed to give them maneuvering room. She had been assigned a station on the starboard side of the dorm "ship," so she knew to stay out of the way and await further instructions.

"I was wondering when Mallet would schedule our next drill," Kathryn remarked, remembering to clip her unruly hair back this time. "Figures he'd wake us up in the middle of the night."

"It's one o'clock," Thrum reported helpfully.

That meant that Kathryn had finished talking to Amelia only five hours ago. Deeply troubled by the experience, she hadn't gone to bed till midnight. She'd had less than an hour's sleep! But she was brimming with energy now as the loudspeaker repeated, *"Red Alert! Port sections to battle stations!"*

Ready in record time, Pol ran for the door. "Wish me luck!" she called back to her twin as she disappeared.

Kathryn hastened after Pol, telling Thrum, "Looks like you've got it easy this time!"

"We'll see," Thrum responded, staring after her vanished twin.

The hallway echoed with the wail of the klaxon and the pounding of feet as cadets ran to their posts. Kathryn hurried to the nearest lift to find Dunkirk and several other cadets waiting for the lift doors to open. Kathryn wondered if Dunkirk was angry with her for how she'd treated him that afternoon, but he didn't act put out. He said hello to her, running a hand through his bed-headed hair a little self-consciously. Then the lift doors opened and everyone piled inside.

Dunkirk gave a loud snort when Hally Coogan dashed into the lift just before the doors shut. Just like the first drill, Coogan's uniform was perfect, his

boots polished, his hair neatly combed. "You've done it again, Coog!" Dunkirk marveled. "What's your secret? Don't you ever sleep?"

"Yeah," said Theda Marr, "during class."

"Ha, ha," Coogan said, smug as ever. "You guys just don't know the secrets of perfection, that's all."

Kathryn itched to ask Coogan what he meant by that, but there was no time. The lift doors opened on the second floor, and she and Dunkirk leaped out and ran for Station 13.

Their station monitor informed them that their "ship" was under Romulan attack. They took several bad phaser "hits," during which Kathryn and Dunkirk had to be sure to keep the bridge supplied with full readouts from the sensor arrays. At one point their console overloaded from an energy surge caused by a hit and they had to perform complicated repairs at top speed. Kathryn was pleased by Dunkirk's efficiency this time. Not only was he cool under pressure, but he was fast. Together they got the repairs completed in mere minutes and sent the delayed sensor data flashing up to the bridge.

Despite his efficiency, however, Dunkirk barely spoke during their work. Kathryn realized she must have hurt his feelings after all. "Good job, Frost," she said afterward, and meant it.

He nodded. "Thanks." That was it. Nothing more.

He's mad at me all right, Kathryn thought. *C'mon, Janeway, you owe him.* Kathryn risked pulling her eyes away from her readout panel so that she could give Dunkirk a smile. But as she did, she noticed Pol run right past Station 13 at full speed. "Pol—?" Kathryn called out in surprise, but the Diasoman didn't answer and didn't stop. She disappeared down the hallway.

"What's with her?" Dunkirk asked, watching Pol's retreating figure.

"I don't know," Kathryn said, "but the drill's not over. She should still be at her post."

"Maybe she got special orders."

"Yeah, maybe." But Kathryn doubted it. Although she'd gotten only a quick look at Pol's face, she'd seen an expression of panic on it. Not the kind of panic that one could associate with a drill scenario, but genuine full-throttle panic. "I'm worried, Frost."

"You're not thinking of following her, are you?" asked Dunkirk in disbelief.

"Something's wrong. I can feel it."

"But the drill's not over!"

"Maybe, but whatever was making Pol run didn't have anything to do with the drill." For an agonized moment Kathryn struggled between concern for her performance grade and concern for Pol. To her surprise, she found herself running down the hallway. "I've got to see if she's all right!" she called back to Dunkirk.

By the time Kathryn found her roommate, the Red Alert lights had stopped flashing. The drill was over. Pol was standing with her sister outside their dorm room, and they were arguing. "You stupid *grizbokkit,*

I'm all right!" Thrum was saying. "It was part of the drill!"

"How was I supposed to know that?" Pol growled defensively. "Next time, don't panic so loud!"

"I didn't panic!"

"Yes, you did! I felt it!"

Kathryn hated to interfere with the twins when they were arguing, but she was in no mood for childish behavior. She physically stepped between them and ordered, "Calm down, both of you!"

For an instant they stopped, glaring angrily at her. Then each of them took a deep breath, ready to continue their argument as if Kathryn weren't there.

Kathryn would have none of it. "Don't say another word!" She turned to Pol. "Now what happened? You ran past my station like a cat on fire."

Pol pointed an accusing finger at her twin. "Thrum sent panic at me. I couldn't help it, I thought she was dying!"

"Sent panic?" Kathryn repeated, looking to Thrum for an explanation.

"You know that Pol and I are linked," Thrum said, and when she tapped her skull to indicate their psychic connection, Pol tapped hers as well, in perfect sync with her twin. "While you two were at your stations," Thrum continued, "our dorm room experienced an atmospheric reduction. I know now that it was part of the drill, simulated damage from the Romulan attack. But for a brief moment I panicked when I couldn't breathe. Then I came to my senses, found my rebreather in our room emergency kit and put it on, just as I would be required to do on a real starship under such circumstances." Her big eyes stared down at the floor, betraying guilt. "I suppose I transmitted my initial panic to Pol without meaning to."

"That's exactly what you did," Pol accused. "It was so strong that I panicked as well. Thanks to you, I left my post. I've surely failed the drill!"

Kathryn said quietly, "Well, I've failed it, too, thanks to both of you."

The Diasomans' mouths dropped open. "Oh, dear," Pol said in shock.

"We're so very sorry," added Thrum earnestly.

Kathryn said nothing, wondering why she wasn't angry with them. The only anger she felt was aimed at herself, and it grew at the sight of CGC Mallet and Ensign Hott coming down the hallway. *I'm sorry, Daddy,* she thought, realizing that the first ugly blot on her perfect Academy record was on its way.

"Cadets Pol, Janeway," said Mallet, stopping before them. "Why did you leave your posts?"

The girls explained what happened, and Mallet listened without showing any reaction. When the story was finished, he merely said, "Cadet Thrum, you performed as required. You may return to bed."

Thrum looked at her roommates with concern. "Sir—"

"You have your orders, cadet," Mallet said firmly.

"Uh . . . yes, sir." Thrum unhappily went into the dorm room and closed the door.

"You two,'" Mallet said to Kathryn and Pol, "come with me to my office." He led them down to the dorm's first floor and on to a small room set off from the Main Lounge. Kathryn couldn't help but notice Mallet's infamous "countdown clock" outside his door. It was nothing but a digital display with a number on it, presently "5." Mallet claimed it represented the number of cadets who had washed out of the Academy so far that semester.

Kathryn had been in Mallet's office before, for a general interview during her first week. She knew to sit in one of the contoured chairs, not on the plush couch in the corner. Mallet crossed to his big oak desk. Hott waited for Mallet's nod, then left the office, closing the door behind him.

Mallet turned to Pol. "Cadet Pol, I don't need to lecture you, do I? You know what you did was wrong and why."

Pol swallowed. "Yes, sir, I do." As she spoke, her left arm twitched, as if she were having some kind of seizure. Kathryn noticed it, and so did Mallet. They'd both seen it before, each time the Diasomans were physically separated. Such twitches were common during the separation process. It was merely a sign of nervousness and would diminish as the twins grew apart. But for now it was painful to watch, especially since Pol looked so miserable already.

Not that Kathryn didn't have her own pain to bear. She was so angry with herself that she was clenching her jaws. The muscles of her neck were beginning to cramp, but she just couldn't relax them. *Good,* she thought. *You deserve to feel bad, Kathryn. You made a stupid mistake and there's no excuse for it.*

As for Mallet, he showed no emotion whatsoever, neither toward Pol nor toward Kathryn. He simply turned to Kathryn. "Cadet Janeway?"

Kathryn tried to look stern and unflappable, the exact opposite of how she felt. "Yes, sir," she managed through gritted teeth.

"As much as I commend your concern for a fellow crew member, you know that I can't commend your performance. As much as our human compassion compels us to act selflessly, such behavior can be disastrous aboard a starship. These dorm drills, and the holosuite tests you'll take throughout your Academy training, are designed to show you when to follow compassion and when to follow logic.

"Space is not compassionate. Sometimes lives are lost. In this case, had tonight's simulation been a real starship situation, you would have endangered yourself and your entire ship by leaving your post to pursue one crew member," and he indicated Pol, "who would have been running into a disaster area. Panicked as she was, Pol may have gotten herself hurt, and perhaps you along with her."

Kathryn said nothing

Mallet moved to his chair, picked up a data padd and punched several keys. The little instrument beeped and booped merrily in contrast to Mallet's next words: "I'm assigning you both to a holosuite test. This test will not make up for tonight's mistakes, nor will a perfect score erase those mistakes from your records. But it will serve, I trust, as a valuable lesson. Report to Training Holosuite Four tomorrow evening after classes. I'll expect you both to return each evening thereafter until you have solved the puzzle to my satisfaction."

"Puzzle, sir?" Kathryn ventured.

"Yes, puzzle." Mallet gestured at the door. "That will be all, cadets. Dismissed."

During the walk back to their room, Kathryn could feel Pol staring at her, as if the Diasoman were hoping she'd say something. But Kathryn had nothing to say and kept her eyes straight ahead. "It was all my fault," Pol finally blurted. "I'm sorry you got involved, Kathryn."

"Pol, you did what you had to do," Kathryn replied. "It had nothing to do with me. I left my post during a Red Alert. If the drill scenario had been real and anything had happened to Dunkirk, our whole ship could have been endangered. I let my emotions run away with me—literally," she finished bitterly.

When they reached their room, they found Dunkirk Frost waiting in the hallway. Everyone else had gone back to bed. Dunkirk looked at Kathryn with concern. "So what happened?" he whispered.

"We got chewed out," Kathryn bluntly whispered back. "Excuse me, I have to get some sleep." She tried to push past him, but Dunkirk didn't budge.

"Kathryn, are you okay?"

LIFELINE

She glared at him. "What does it matter to you, Frost? My mistake won't reflect on your performance." With a deliberate shove, she got past him and entered her room.

Kathryn quietly put her pajamas back on, careful not to awaken Thrum. As she crawled back into bed, she could hear Pol and Dunkirk still talking quietly outside. Part of her wanted to find out what they were talking about, but the angry part of her swallowed up all curiosity and replaced it with cold determination. *If Mallet's holosuite puzzle is a punishment, then he'll see it solved so fast it'll look like a vacation,* she vowed to herself.

But even her determination couldn't compensate for the terrible disappointment she felt in herself. Replaying her mistake over and over in her mind, Kathryn didn't fall asleep till nearly dawn.

Chapter

7

With a flash of light, the planet exploded.

"Blast it!" Kathryn cried, watching gargantuan chunks of planetary debris whip past her viewscreen, tumbling end-over-end in their weightless flight. "I monitored the readouts. The levels were within tolerable limits. What happened this time?"

Pol stood nearby, her arm twitching, a frown on her face. Her eyes flicked across the readouts. "Well, the planetary substation command signal acknowledgments slipped out of phase with the main data stream, for one. Then, the geothermal levels kept bouncing in and out of safety tolerances even though they averaged out as safe. The fail-safe shutdown routines weren't implemented because the coordinating proces- sor wasn't getting real-time data-flow anymore and . . ." Pol's voice faltered at the grim look on Kathryn's face. "It's a lot to keep track of," she said, almost apologetically.

"Not for me," said Kathryn. "Computer, freeze sim- ulation." The planetary debris on screen froze in place, and all instrumentation froze as well. "Mallet said this was a puzzle. There must be some trick I haven't thought of yet, that's all."

Kathryn stood at the central console in the Emitter Control Room of the starship *Argonaut,* but in reality the control room was the transformed interior of a holosuite at the campus Holo Center. She and Pol had been there for two hours already, and so far they'd done nothing but fail.

This was the Academy's infamous Gravitation Reg- ulation Station Epsilon program, otherwise known as the GRSE, or GREASY test. Its scenario was simple. As described by the computer itself: "You are science technicians aboard the starship *U.S.S. Argonaut* or- biting planet Epsilon One, a class-M world with an advanced humanoid population of 3.76 billion. Gaussian field instabilities in the planet's core will soon cause massive tectonic and volcanic activity, threatening the population with annihilation. Your ship's science officer has worked out a plan to utilize the onboard warp generators to seal the planetary core in a containment bubble and to use a combina- tion of surface substations and the ship's controls to stabilize Epsilon One's core field. Your responsibility as leader of the stabilization team is to supervise the establishment of the containment bubble and coordinate interaction of the shipboard and dirtside field manipulations. Your efforts will determine whether the stabilization is accomplished safely. Good luck."

It had all sounded quite straightforward to Kathryn until she got her first look at the process flow diagrams. With a dozen planetary substations exchanging data with the shipboard computer at near-light speed, the stabilization process would push the envelope of a *Miranda*-class vessel's capabilities. There were hundreds of field manipulation points that had to flux in near-perfect synch and at least a thousand variables that could fluctuate and reduce the whole process to chaos—a chaos that could doom billions of people in mere minutes.

Now, four attempts and 15.04 billion deaths later, the only thing that proved straightforward was how quickly Kathryn could fail each time. Curtly, she snapped commands to the holocomputer.

"Computer, run GREASY scenario again, but skip the intro. Start at the beginning of the stabilization process."

The computer chirped obligingly and the control room shimmered. When it reappeared it was the same as before, except the instrument readouts were different and the viewscreen showed a blue, cloud-flecked planet below.

Pol had sat uselessly by Kathryn's side all this time,

waiting for her team leader to give her tasks to fulfil. But Kathryn's ruthless focus on the simulation had seemingly rendered the Diasoman invisible. Beyond that, Pol had never been separated from Thrum for so long before, and the strain was beginning to show. Not only was her arm twitching, but her normally cheery disposition had slipped into depression. "What do you want me to do?" she ventured hesitantly.

"As soon as I understand what needs to be done, I'll let you know," Kathryn muttered, eyes jumping from readout to readout.

Pol might have said something in response, but Kathryn wasn't listening anymore. Her fingers flew like lightning across the control surfaces, setting up a new solution to cope with the ever-changing core conditions. With a process that could shift faster than a human could follow, Kathryn was convinced that her best solution was to try to anticipate what might go wrong and have adjustment routines preloaded and ready for execution. She tightened the feedback loop between the ship and the ground stations, then signaled the bridge. "Emitter Control standing by."

"Acknowledged, Emitter Control," came the voice of the science officer over the comm. "Initialize stabilization process."

"Initializing stabilization process Janeway Mark Five."

All around Kathryn, the readouts began to change more rapidly. She looked quickly from one to the other and tapped various controls, shifting massive energy flows as fast as she could.

"Emitter Control, substations Three, Seven and Twelve are failing and dropping off-line. Geothermal levels are redlining," came the voice over the comm. "Decrease flow stream. Compensate immediately!"

Sweat beaded Kathryn's brow, dripping into her eyes as she flicked them from readout to readout. "Aye, aye," she acknowledged, trying desperately to stem the rising tide of red lights. There were just too many controls to handle at once!

"Stations One, Two and Nine report field-compression backlash," warned the science officer, more urgent this time. "They're gone, Emitter Control! Destroyed! Abort stabilization process at once!"

"Wait a minute," Kathryn stammered, "I'm almost—"

"Overload imminent!" shouted the comm speaker. "She's going to—"

The viewscreen image of Epsilon One exploded. Seconds later, a blinding flash of light enveloped Kathryn. When she could see again, the simulated Emitter Control Room was gone and the black-and-yellow gridded walls of the holosuite surrounded her and Pol.

"Epsilon One has been destroyed," reported the computer's bland voice. "U.S.S. Argonaut has been destroyed."

"Oh, great," moaned Kathryn. "This time I not only blew up the planet, I blew up my own ship as well."

Calling it quits for the night, Kathryn and Pol left

the Holo Center and headed back to the dorms. Kathryn grumbled as she walked, telling Pol everything that had just happened as if the Diasoman hadn't been there with her the whole time. She was just thinking out loud, trying to figure out a new angle on the problem, when she noticed Pol's pace getting faster and faster. "Pol, calm down. I know you've been separated from Thrum for over two hours, but—"

Pol broke into a run. Kathryn raced after her, all the way up the dorm steps, through the Main Lounge and up to their room. Pol burst through the door and threw herself into her sister's arms. "Thrum!"

Thrum held her sister tight. "Pol, you're back! What took you so long? I thought I was going to twitch myself into a fit!"

"It's my fault," Kathryn said, flopping down on her bed. "I took too long on the GREASY test. And I failed."

Pol pulled reluctantly away from her twin. "It wasn't your fault, Kathryn. I should have helped."

"You had enough on your mind already," Kathryn said.

"I will handle it better tomorrow," Pol promised. "Thrum and I—"

"—both will," finished Thrum. "Functioning on our own becomes easier—"

"—as time goes by. The trick is—"

"—to keep moving forward and not look back."

In other words, just keep running, Kathryn thought, getting tired just thinking about it. *Don't worry about where you're running to, just run.* She pulled herself up to a sitting position. "Well, girls, I have some studying to do before I hit the sack."

Pol giggled. "Hit the sack. I love that expression!"

"It makes no sense," Thrum stated critically. "We cadets do not sleep in sacks, and even if we did, why hit them first?"

Pol punched Thrum's arm. "Who cares? It's funny."

A knock on the door interrupted them. Kathryn said, "Come in," and the door *whooshed* aside to reveal Dunkirk Frost. Kathryn jumped to her feet. "Like I said, I've gotta go," she told the twins, and before Dunkirk could utter a word, she grabbed up her data packs and headed out the door, squeezing past Dunkirk with a too-cheery, "Hi, Frost. See ya later."

Kathryn hurried down the hallway, trying not to think about why she'd needed to escape from Dunkirk Frost. Being around him bothered her lately, although she certainly didn't dislike him. She liked him a lot. But every time he came around, she felt anxious. She preferred not to ponder what that might mean.

Pushing the anxiety aside, Kathryn focused her mind on the problem at hand. She wasn't really going to study, per se. She wanted to go over her memories of the GREASY test and analyze the scenario. Already she'd failed it five times, all in the first evening. Mallet would no doubt receive a record of her attempts from the Holo Center in the morning, so he'd know each mistake she made and how many times she repeated them. *I've got to attack this thing from a completely different angle tomorrow,* she thought. *I've got to demonstrate an ability to change my tactics when my first attempts fail. Otherwise I'll just come across as stubborn and unimaginative, and that's a very poor combination for a future Starfleet officer.*

Kathryn spent three hours going over the problem, and she didn't get to bed until two o'clock the next morning.

For the twenty-seventh time, Epsilon One exploded.

Kathryn pounded her fist down hard on her console. "Computer, again!" She didn't have to supply a precise explanation of what she wanted anymore. The holosuite computer had repeated her command so many times now that it automatically returned her to the same scenario at the same place.

Each readout shimmered back to its starting point, and Epsilon One popped back into existence on the viewscreen. Kathryn unclenched her fist, made a quick note on a data padd, then opened her mouth to say, "Begin."

Nothing came out. No words, no sound, not even a squeak. Kathryn stood there with her mouth hanging open and nothing happened. All around her instrumentation, gauges, readouts and viewscreens stood frozen in holotime, waiting for the command to imitate reality. But Kathryn Janeway couldn't give the command. Slowly she sank into a chair, dazed. Her fingers grew numb, and her data padd clattered to the floor.

A full week had passed since Mallet had assigned Kathryn and Pol the GREASY test, and over that week Kathryn had pondered the puzzle every spare moment she had. Pol tried her best to work with her each evening in the holosuite, but Kathryn didn't want the Diasoman's help. "If the dorm drill had been real, I could have destroyed an entire starship full of people," she kept telling Pol. "I don't deserve any help with this. I've got to do it myself." Pol tried to remind her that the test had been assigned to both of them, but Kathryn was so obsessed now that she wouldn't listen.

At one point Kathryn had concluded that the test must be unsolvable, and she'd reported that to Mallet. He'd only looked at her with one side of his mouth quirked up. "No, Cadet Janeway, there is a solution," he had assured her. "You just have to find it."

"With all due respect, sir, it's not there," Kathryn had boldly insisted.

With equal insistence, Mallet had repeated, "There is a solution, cadet. That's all I'm going to say."

After that, Kathryn started to come to the holosuite alone. She was going to find the solution if it killed her. When she finally triumphed, she would share the solution with Pol and they would both be rid of this maddening burden. Yet tonight was her third solo trip and things seemed as hopeless as ever. GREASY was just one brick wall Kathryn couldn't seem to climb.

Heaving a sigh born of depression as much as fatigue, Kathryn pulled herself to her feet. "Computer, arch," she commanded. As if by magic, the holosuite's arched exit appeared. Slipping a hand into her pocket, Kathryn pulled out a program chip and placed it into a secondary input slot of the arch's control panel. "Computer, superimpose additional program Kathryn One, with modifications."

Nothing happened.

"Computer, I said run additional program."

"I'm over here," came a familiar voice.

Kathryn turned to find Amelia Earhart, not two feet tall, standing in the far corner. "Is this some kind of a joke, kid?" Amelia asked, hands on hips, eyes narrow.

Kathryn's nerves snapped. She burst into laughter, pointing at Amelia, and collapsed into a chair. Amelia folded her arms and just stood there, tapping one foot. "I'm sorry," Kathryn gasped, chuckling, "but I just didn't expect—"

"—a Munchkin, I know," Amelia finished. "My program isn't compatible with this GREASY simulation. It put a glitch in my code, if you'd care to fix it."

Kathryn's chuckles subsided. "I don't have time, Amelia, and it doesn't really matter how tall you are. I just need to talk to you."

"Well, I need to see something besides your shins," Amelia retorted.

Kathryn picked her holo-friend up and placed her on a console. "Better?"

"It'll do." Amelia straightened her leather aviator's jacket. "So what's up?"

Kathryn spoke almost too cheerfully, with an edge

of hysteria in her voice. "I'm cracking up, Amelia. I don't know what's happening anymore. I mean, no matter how hard I try, I fail. No matter how focused I am, everything's a blur." She threw her hands in the air. "I don't know what I'm doing anymore!"

Amelia said nothing. In fact, she turned her back on Kathryn, gazing around the Emitter Control Room with an expression of awe, peering into readout screens as big as she was and gingerly fingering control pads that were so sensitive they could have responded to her miniature touch if the GREASY program had been running.

Kathryn frowned. "Amelia, pay attention!"

Amelia calmly turned back around. "I'm listening. You're complaining because you can't solve a little problem by yourself. Well, let me tell you something, kid—flying solo isn't easy. It never was. I should know. If you think it's hard now, wait until your problems are *real.* No"—Amelia turned back to fingering a console curiously—"you need a little perspective, I think."

Kathryn's face flushed red with anger. "All right, then give it to me."

"You can't just *give* somebody perspective," said Amelia. "C'mon, Kathryn, step back and take a look at yourself. From what I can see, you've put more emphasis on *achieving* goals than on *why* you want to achieve those goals. Just tell me something—what are you here for?"

"I'm trying to solve this stupid test!"

"No, I mean Starfleet Academy. Why are you here?"

Kathryn blinked. "I want a career in Starfleet," she answered reasonably.

"But *why?*"

As if this simple question were as much of a test as GREASY itself, Kathryn kicked into overdrive, struggling to compose a perfect response. "I want a life of adventure," she declared. "I want to explore places nobody's ever been before, see things nobody's ever seen before. I mean, some of the Starfleet stories that Daddy used to tell me when I was a little . . ." Her voice trailed off.

"Go on," Amelia prodded.

But Kathryn couldn't speak. *Daddy,* she thought, wondering.

Amelia broke the silence. "Kid, you're not falling apart. You're just trying too hard to do too much. You're only one person, and there are only twenty-four hours in a day. You can only accomplish so much. That was a fact even in my time." She glanced at the tiny watch on her wrist. "And speaking of time, it's almost five o'clock—dinner in the mess hall, if I'm not mistaken."

Kathryn's thoughts were more confused now than ever before. "So?"

"So go eat a decent meal and don't eat it alone. Sit with somebody, for goodness sake. Talk to somebody *real.*" Amelia finished with emphasis, "Give yourself a break, kid, before *you* break. Okay? Promise me?"

Kathryn nodded. "Okay, okay."

Amelia jabbed a finger at the arch's control panel. "Now turn me off. I hate being small."

"Computer," Kathryn said, "end program Kathryn One."

Amelia waved as she faded away.

For an instant, Kathryn thought of trying the GREASY just one more time, but she'd given her word, even if it was to a hologram. She turned off the test program and went to have dinner with a friend. *If I have any left,* she thought glumly.

Chapter

8

Kathryn finished eating dinner and placed her tray on the recycle shelf. It disappeared in a sparkling spiral of energy, its molecular components ready to be recombined to make a new, clean, replicated place setting later.

Kathryn had eaten alone. She'd walked hopefully if not confidently into the mess hall for dinner only to discover that she didn't know a single person there. Rallying her courage, she'd gone to her room to fetch ThrumPol but they were out. Dunkirk wasn't in his room either. Even Hally Coogan was out. Though she knew she should have tried to make a new friend, Kathryn had decided to eat alone. Again.

Thanks for the advice, Amelia, she thought sourly as she returned to her room afterward. *Now I feel worse than I did before.* Kathryn sat down at her study desk, anxious to lose herself in homework, when she noticed the comm padd on her desk blinking. It was a message from CGC Mallet: "Report immediately to my office." *He must have checked my performance on the GREASY test. I doubt he's pleased.* Steeling herself for a reprimand, Kathryn headed for his office.

Once there, she activated the door chime, noticing Mallet's countdown clock as she did so. The number read 8 now. *Three more cadets have washed out since I started the GREASY test,* she thought. *Will I make it nine . . . ?*

"Come," said a stern voice from inside the office. The door opened to reveal CGC Mallet seated behind his desk. "Ah, Cadet Janeway. Come in, please."

The more polite and friendly Mallet was, the worse the news he had to give. That was how it seemed to work anyway. Kathryn walked in, more nervous than before, and sat in one of the contoured chairs. Mallet cleared his throat, as if preparing himself for something unpleasant. "I'm disappointed in you, cadet," he said.

Kathryn gulped. "Sir?"

"I'd been given to understand that you were a bright, energetic, enthusiastic and honest individual."

Kathryn wanted to say, "I am!" but obviously Mallet already thought differently.

He explained. "I accessed your GREASY performance records from the holosuite center this afternoon and noticed that a second program had been superimposed on it for approximately five minutes. Exactly what was this program?"

Amelia! He found a trace of Amelia! Kathryn wasn't simply startled or even embarrassed—she slipped into full-scale panic. *If he finds out about her, I'll be the laughingstock of the Academy!* It took all of Kathryn's willpower to keep her voice steady. "I can explain, sir."

"Please do."

"It was . . ." Kathryn struggled as her voice threatened to quit on her. ". . . a personal program, sir."

"Personal in what way?"

"It was something I brought from home."

Kathryn cringed as Mallet's eyes grew dark. "Let's cut to the chase, Cadet Janeway. Were you using a program simulation aid?"

"Sir!" The word leaped from Kathryn's mouth like a shot from an old-style pistol. So this was Mallet's concern. He suspected her of *cheating!* "I am not a cheater, sir," she assured him.

"Then what was that program?"

Cornered, Kathryn reluctantly explained how she'd modified a counseling program years ago, about how Amelia had helped her over the years, and how she'd brought Amelia with her to Starfleet Academy. Mallet listened without showing any reaction, but Kathryn herself felt like a fool by the time her story was finished.

Mallet sighed, and his mask of nonreaction slipped. It revealed disappointment. Not just a little, but a lot, as if he felt personally betrayed. The look reminded Kathryn of her father when he was disappointed in her. For Kathryn, nothing was worse than disappointing her father. "The Academy can't have its officers-in-training running to their imaginary friends when things get tough," Mallet said after a moment. "You will bring me the Amelia program chip immediately, and I will return it to you after you have graduated . . . *if* you graduate. Until that time, I suggest that if you feel a need for counseling, you make an appointment with an Academy professional. Do I make myself clear?"

Kathryn wanted to run away, to hide, to do anything but feel the hot wave of embarrassment that coursed through her body. "Yes, sir," she said softly.

"That will be all, cadet. Dismissed."

Moving as quickly as she could without actually running, Kathryn left the room.

Two days later, Kathryn felt worse than ever. Without Amelia to turn to, she felt isolated from everyone, alone even in a room full of people. Like a robot she could carry on a conversation, but throughout such moments she felt as if she were trapped in a bubble, trying to break through some invisible nightmarish boundary that kept her from really connecting with anyone around her. Thanks to her own Prime Directive, Kathryn had pushed her peers so far away she couldn't reach them anymore.

When she wasn't in class, she spent her time in the GREASY simulation. If nothing else, she had to convince Mallet she wasn't a quitter. But whatever the CGC thought of her efforts, those efforts were making Kathryn's relationship with ThrumPol nearly intolerable. That afternoon as she approached her room, she heard them talking inside. "Pol, this has gone far enough. You must tell Mallet. You two are supposed to be working on the test together, and instead Kathryn is doing it all by herself—and failing! It's making you look bad."

Kathryn didn't stay long enough to hear Pol's reply.

That evening, she avoided her room and escaped to the Study Lounge to cram for an astronavigation exam. She was so exhausted after several hours of fighting GREASY, however, that she fell asleep within minutes. Vaguely she heard cadets come and go, keeping their voices low so as not to disturb their studying, or sleeping, peers. Then one voice broke through to Kathryn's consciousness: "There she is."

Kathryn opened one eye and spotted ThrumPol standing in the doorway of the Study Lounge, staring right at her. Thrum was frowning while Pol fidgeted nervously. Kathryn's first impulse was to close her eye, remain motionless and hope they went away. But Thrum started forward, pulling Pol after her. At a loss to know how to handle the situation, Kathryn feigned sleep until the Diasomans were standing in front of her. "Kathryn," came Thrum's firm voice.

Kathryn opened her eyes, pretending that she'd just awakened. "Hm?"

"May we sit down?"

"Uh . . . sure." Kathryn knew what was going to happen and dreaded it. *You saw it coming,* she thought. *Now there's no way out.*

ThrumPol sat down. "We need to talk—" Thrum began.

"—about the GREASY test," finished Pol reluctantly.

"And other things as well. The fact is, Kathryn—"

A new voice broke in. "Kathryn! There you are!"

Kathryn was never so glad to see Dunkirk Frost as she was at that moment. Why he wanted to even speak to her at this point was a mystery, but at least his appearance was cutting short a conversation that Kathryn didn't want to have. Other cadets in the room stared as he hurried over to her table, but they went back to studying when Dunkirk plunked himself down in a chair and said in a barely audible whisper, "I have news!"

Clearly Thrum didn't appreciate this interruption, but Pol smiled at the young man. "What is it?"

Dunkirk leaned close. "I found out Sleepless Coogan's secret. You know, why he's always perfectly dressed for a surprise drill?" He leaned in even closer and whispered even more softly, so softly that Kathryn had to strain to hear. "He sleeps in his uniform! Not

only that, but he sleeps above his bedcovers! If there's a drill, he just leaps up, combs his hair and goes! If there's an inspection, all he has to do is straighten his covers and he's set!''

Thrum was interested now. She exchanged a glance with Pol. "So that's—"

"—how he does it. How did you—"

"—find out?"

"That's between me and modern technology," said Dunkirk with a sly wink. "Let's just say I've been keeping an eye on Mister Perfect for some time."

"Does Coogan know?" Thrum asked.

"The question is, does *Mallet* know?" said Pol.

"No and no," answered Dunkirk. "I think." He turned to Kathryn. "Pretty good, eh, Kathryn? Now we can do the same thing. No more drills with wrinkled uniforms and magneto-hair. Don't thank me too much, though, I embarrass easily." He grinned at her expectantly.

All Kathryn could do was yawn. She was so tired she could hardly sit up straight. "Thanks, Frost," she slurred. "Really." She shook her head, feeling dizzy. "I'm sorry, you guys, but I have to rest a minute." The next thing she knew, her head was cradled in her arms, which were folded on the tabletop. Tingles of sleep threatened to carry her away . . .

Dunkirk's smile faded. With her eyes closed Kathryn couldn't actually see it happen, but somehow she felt it. *Kathryn, Frost just gave you a wonderful gift,* she realized, *and you took it with nothing more than a slurry, monotoned thank-you!* Through a haze of sleepiness her brain finally registered just how impolite—how insensitive!—she'd become.

Kathryn raised her head and opened her mouth to speak, intending to apologize to Dunkirk, but he was already walking away. Before she could call him back Pol popped up from her chair and trotted after him. Kathryn watched as the normally hesitant Diasoman boldly took Dunkirk's arm and pulled him to one side. The two of them started whispering to each other.

Maybe it was the Study Lounge's acoustics. Maybe it was the fact that the cadets in the lounge were all studying quietly. Or maybe it was just a nasty quirk of fate. Whatever the reason, Kathryn could hear what Pol and Dunkirk were saying, though just barely. She knew Thrum could hear them, too.

"Don't feel bad," Pol said. "I'm sure she likes you."

"Yeah, right," Dunkirk replied sullenly. "Pol, I feel like a total idiot. I've tried to be nice to her, but Kathryn's so wrapped up in school she's not even in our universe anymore. I'm wasting my time."

Dunkirk's words hit Kathryn like a slap in the face. "Dunkirk *likes* me?" she blurted.

"You didn't know?" asked Thrum, a distinct tinge of sarcasm to her tone.

"Well, no, I mean . . ." Kathryn's head spun. It must have been obvious to everyone else in the universe but her, how Dunkirk kept asking her out to holopics and concerts and how he always acted so concerned about the events in her life. He really cared! And all she'd done was repeatedly brush him aside.

As if that weren't bad enough, Pol was actually defending Kathryn. After the way Kathryn had treated her, Pol was still trying to help! Even Thrum, angry as she was with Kathryn, had the grace not to gloat. Quite the contrary, the Diasoman sat gazing at her with an expression of pity more than anything else.

Kathryn felt worse than she'd ever felt in her life. *You've made a botch of things, Kathryn. Somehow you've got to straighten everything out, and you've got to do it right now!*

That's when the klaxon went off.

Chapter

9

"Red Alert! Red Alert! All hands to battle stations!"

Every cadet in the study lounge leaped to their feet. What happened next took them all by surprise—their feet left the floor! "The gravity's out!" Pol squealed.

Everyone slowly floated upward until they were hanging helplessly in midair, eyes wide in shock, mouths gaping. The Study Lounge tables, like most furniture in the dorm, were bolted in place, so they stayed put. However, chairs, data packs, jackets, pillows and every other unsecured item rose gently upward, creating a floating obstacle course of debris. "I've never been in zero-g before!" Cadet Lisa Kearny yelled, trying to make herself heard over the still-blaring klaxon. "What do we do now?"

"How do we get to our posts?" someone else in the floating crowd complained

"Swim for it!" Kearny suggested. She started flapping her arms about, trying to maneuver herself down so she could grab the lip of the table, but her weightless gyrations only sent her into an uncontrolled tumble in the opposite direction. "Help!" she cried as her arm struck a floating data pack and sent it sailing across the room where it smacked someone else in the forehead.

"Ouch!" the victim yelped.

Flailing helplessly, Kearny's arm bumped someone to her right and her leg kicked someone to her left. Those cadets were knocked into their own spins, and before long, half the cadets in the room were slowly tumbling head-over-heels, helpless to do anything about it. The errant data pack continued to sail through the air, bouncing against walls and cadets until Theda Marr caught it with her feet.

"Everybody stop flapping around and just relax!" Kathryn called, putting as much authority as she could into her voice. Just her luck she was stuck in a room full of space newbies. Kathryn had experienced zero-g several times, thanks to her father's position in Starfleet. She knew that maneuvering without any weight or leverage was difficult but not impossible. "The best thing to do is grab a stationary object, but do it *slowly!*"

"I'm going to throw up!" threatened one of the spinners.

"Oh, don't, please," Dunkirk begged.

"Everybody calm down," repeated Kathryn. "I'll try to reach the bookshelf and clear this whole mess up." Slowly, so that she didn't send herself into a helpless spin as well, Kathryn stretched out one arm. Her fingertips were a mere two inches from the edge of the bookcase, but there was no way for her to propel herself forward. With an angry growl she stretched her whole body, trying like mad to grow two inches so she could touch that bookcase, but it was simply out of reach.

Then a little voice in Kathryn's head said, *Flying solo isn't easy, kid. If you think it's hard now, wait until your problems are* real.

Kathryn gasped as a sudden realization dawned on her. *Flying solo,* she thought. *Is that what I've been trying to do?*

Theda Marr's sharp voice yanked Kathryn out of her reverie. "This is ridiculous! Nobody can reach anything! Mallet's going to find us hanging in here like a bunch of jerks!"

"No, he's not," Kathryn said, her vision clear now for the first time since arriving at the Academy."Not if we work *together.*" She twisted around until she could see Thrum. "Take my hand."

Thrum hesitated. "Why?"

"Look, I know you're mad at me," said Kathryn,

"and you have every right to be. But right now we need to work together for everyone's benefit."

Thrum slowly stretched out her hand. Turning carefully, Kathryn barely managed to touch the furry fingertips. "Okay, now gently push me over to the wall."

Thrum pushed Kathryn away. In doing so, she also propelled herself back to the opposite wall. Both Kathryn and Thrum gently hit the flat surfaces, then kicked off again and floated across the room, pushing against the other cadets until everyone had been maneuvered to a wall or piece of stationary furniture. The spinning cadets righted themselves, sighing with relief.

Barely a minute had passed since the klaxon started to ring, but one minute wasted in a drill was far too long. Kathryn knew they had to move fast. "Everybody, listen up!" she said. "My father told me about a zero-g trick he learned in space. Now everybody hold hands!"

Within moments, the Study Lounge cadets had formed a long "body chain" and were hurling each other down the hallways to their stations. Since the hallways were bare, no loose objects created obstacles, so the technique was safe and it quickly caught on. Soon cadets were zipping through the air on every floor, reaching their posts with record speed.

Kathryn decided to throw all caution to the wind and grabbed Dunkirk's arm, grinning at him. "Okay, Frost, let's get to our station."

He looked at her with surprise, but he didn't pull away. "Uh—right!"

They hurled each other down the corridor, dodging their floating peers, as the klaxon continued to howl. "Get in here!" called Hally Coogan, pulling them into the lift.

Other cadets struggled to float inside as Kathryn said to Coogan, "Well, look who's not the only one wearing a uniform this time." She grinned at him, adding, "Get used to it, Coog." Then she winked at Dunkirk. He stared back, obviously wondering at the sudden change in her attitude.

Suddenly Kathryn's grin faded as the lift doors closed. Realization dawned too late. "Wait a minute, don't—!" She began.

But someone activated the lift and it started its swift descent. In that instant, every cadet floating in the small cubicle was smashed up against the ceiling. Except for Kathryn, they were all caught by surprise, and in their haste to orient themselves, they only managed to get caught in a tangle. By the time the lift stopped, the cadets were a compressed knot of arms and legs, bruised shins and snagged hair. "Leggo by dose!" came a nasal cry from somewhere in the floating mass.

"Get your boot out of my face!" yelled somebody else.

"Stop pulling on my arm!" shouted a third. "It's not supposed to bend that way!"

Kathryn was floating free from the waist up, but her legs were still tangled in with everybody else. "Dunkirk, where are you?" She tried to twist around and find him, but somebody's head blocked her view.

Then she heard him giggle. It had to be Dunkirk. Only he could possibly find this disaster amusing. "Wow, some crackerjack Starfleet cadets we are!" he cackled, laughing harder.

The sound of it was contagious. Other cadets started to laugh, and in seconds the whole floating, writhing mass of tangled teenagers was shrieking with hilarity.

Everyone, that is, except Kathryn. "This isn't funny!" she shouted at them, still struggling to pull her legs free. "We've got to get to our stations! Don't you people realize the gravity of the situation?"

All laughter stopped dead, leaving Kathryn's words hanging in the air as much as the cadets themselves. "The gravity of the situation?" came Dunkirk's voice. "The *gravity* . . . ?" He broke into laughter again, and everybody followed suit.

Kathryn blinked. A giggle escaped her. "Gravity of the situation . . ." Another giggle slipped out. "I can't believe I said that . . . the *gravity* of . . ." She started to laugh. Her laughter grew, and the more she tried to stop, the harder she ended up laughing.

Her fellow cadets weren't perfect, that was for sure, but neither was she. Kathryn laughed with them. She laughed at them. She laughed at herself. She laughed so hard she feared her stomach muscles were going to snap.

Instead something else snapped—the holocam in Ensign Hott's hands. He was peeking around the corner into the lift and aiming the camera at them. "Say cheese!" he said, and snapped another holopic.

Through tears of laughter, Kathryn noticed that Hott was standing firmly on the floor. He must have been wearing a pair of gravity boots. Also, the klaxon wasn't blaring anymore. Even the Red Alert lights in the hallway had stopped flashing. "The drill's over," Hott told them. "Prepare yourselves for normalization of environment."

With a burst of efficiency that startled Kathryn, the cadets untangled themselves and maneuvered their bodies head up, feet down. When the gravity returned, they all dropped gently to the floor. "Ta-daah!" Dunkirk said jovially.

Hott pointed a blue finger at him. "See how funny it all is when Mallet hears about this," he warned. "All cadets report to the Study Lounge immediately."

"What are you going to do with the pictures?" Theda Marr asked, indicating Hott's holocam.

Hott patted the camera. "These are for the yearbook. I knew you guys would take the lift in zero-g. Somebody always does."

Mallet was waiting for them in the Study Lounge. The place was a mess, with chairs and study gear strewn about. Cadets picked items up at random as they entered, clearing enough space for everyone to gather for what Kathryn assumed would be a big lecture. "This ought to be fun," Pol growled softly.

Dunkirk patted her arm. "Calm down, Pol. Your hackles are rising."

Contrary to Pol's fears, Mallet didn't lecture them at all, even the cadets who took the lift. "Taking a lift in zero-g is about as stupid a mistake as is possible to make," he told them flatly, "but every year, someone makes it. This class, in fact, will forever carry the distinction of having the most zero-g-ignorant cadets in quite a few years."

Someone actually had the nerve to applaud. When nobody joined in, the clapping awkwardly stopped. "Cadet Coogan," boomed Mallet, "you will see me in my office afterward."

Hally Coogan automatically hid his hands behind his back. "Y-yes, sir," he choked.

Kathryn liked Sleepless Coogan, but she couldn't help but grin. *So much for perfection,* she thought with a wicked sense of satisfaction. *Maybe we should call him Clapper Coogan from now on.*

"It's easy to forget the simple rules of logic in an emergency situation," Mallet continued. "That's why we have drills. I suggest we keep our wits about us next time." One side of his mouth quirked up. "That is all, cadets. Dismissed!"

Everyone headed back to their rooms, but Kathryn had to find her study materials first. As she poked through piles of debris, she was joined by Dunkirk, Thrum and Pol. "So, Janeway, back there in the elevator—that was the first joke I've ever heard you make," said Dunkirk. "It was pretty funny. You never told me you had a sense of humor."

"You never asked," Kathryn replied.

Dunkirk shrugged. "Gee, I didn't know I had to."

"You didn't." Kathryn rallied her courage and said what should have been said days earlier. "Look, all of you, I . . . that is . . . well . . ."

"You want to apologize—" began Pol.

"—for being a *grizbokkit,*" finished Thrum helpfully.

Kathryn's eyebrows shot up. "I haven't been that bad! Have I?"

"Worse," Dunkirk said. "Infinitely worse." He turned to the twins. "What's a *grizbokkit?*"

Kathryn took a blind stab at a definition. "Somebody who's a foolish, pigheaded spoiler," she said. ThrumPol nodded that she was in the general ballpark. "I'm sorry for being one, I really am," Kathryn went on. "I just lost perspective." Her voice tried to give out on her, but she vowed never to let that old bad habit come back again. She forced the words out. "Will you . . . forgive me?"

Dunkirk folded his arms and glanced at the twins. "How about it, cadets? Should we forgive her?"

ThrumPol screwed up their faces as if calculating a highly complex math equation in their heads. Then they said in perfect unison, "All right, you are hereby forgiven."

"Just do us one favor," said Dunkirk. "Put superwoman away. Life can be just as challenging but a whole lot easier if you let somebody else help once in a while, you know."

. . . *help once in a while,* thought Kathryn, *help once in a . . .* "That's it!" she cried. "Holy cow, *that's it!*"

"*What's* it?" Dunkirk asked.

"You were right! I'm a bone fide first-class *grizbok-kit!*" And with that, Kathryn grabbed Pol's hands and started running after Mallet.

Mallet heard them coming and turned around. "Cadets, you have been dismissed," he said sternly.

"Sorry, sir," said Kathryn, breathless, "but I've got it! I mean, I *think* I've got it. Pol and I request permission to go to the Holo Center, sir."

Mallet's brows drew together. "Now?"

"Yes, sir."

"What for?" Pol asked, as mystified as Mallet.

"Because," Kathryn told them, "I know the answer to the GREASY test!"

Chapter

10

Cadet Group Commander Mallet stared at Kathryn with that look in his eye, the same look he'd used the first time they'd met. As she had then, Kathryn felt as if the man were drilling a hole straight into her brain with his eyes so that he could examine her thoughts firsthand. "You want to try your solution now, fifteen minutes before the Holo Center closes?" he asked.

"Yes, sir." Kathryn squeezed Pol's hand a little tighter. "We do."

Pol took one look at Kathryn's determined expression and said simply, "Right."

One side of Mallet's mouth quirked up. "Very well, then. Permission granted."

Kathryn rocketed out the door so fast that Pol had to run to catch up with her. "So what's the solution?" the Diasoman demanded. "And why do we have to do it now?"

"I'll explain everything when we get there," Kathryn replied. "As for why we have to do it now, well—there's no time like the present!"

They reached the Holo Center and, because of the late hour, easily found an empty suite. After quickly setting the program, Kathryn found herself standing in the Emitter Control Room of the starship *Argonaut* for the thirty-sixth, and hopefully last, time. "Okay," she said to Pol, "listen carefully. I have discovered that one great characteristic of the *grizbokkit* is its amazing inability to see the obvious, even if the obvious is sitting right in front of its face waving a flag."

Pol giggled but said nothing.

"As much as I'd like to conquer the world all by myself, I have to accept that it can't be done. Not as far as this test is concerned, anyway." Kathryn gestured to herself. "This *grizbokkit* will now assume her post at the Team Leader console, and she requests that you take your post as the Team. *Together,*" said Kathryn, emphasizing the word, "I believe we can solve this thing. What do you say?"

Pol's arm suddenly twitched. Her grin faded. "I'll do my best," she said, hesitation creeping into her voice.

Kathryn placed her hand on the Diasoman's arm. "Pol, we have a job to do, and it has to be done despite how we both feel. If you don't crumble without Thrum's support, I won't try to run the whole show. Agreed?"

The muscles in Pol's arm relaxed. Summoning her resolve, she nodded. "Agreed."

"Right." Kathryn glanced at her chrono. "We've got seven minutes to do this before the Holo Center closes. Let's get it right the first time. Computer, run program!"

Slowly, majestically, the serene blue sphere of Epsilon One began to rotate on the viewscreen. Readouts throughout the simulated control room sprang to life, softly chirping and beeping. Kathryn's eyes raced over her telltales, taking in all the variables and readying herself for the onslaught of activity that would occur once the routine was underway. She fought the impulse to glance over her shoulder to check Pol's console readouts as well, summoning all her willpower to keep her attention focused on her own work. *Trust her, Kathryn,* she commanded herself. *You're not flying solo anymore.*

"I'm ready," came Pol's voice, firm with confidence.

"Acknowledged." Kathryn braced herself, then said, "Bridge, Emitter Control Room standing by."

"Acknowledged, Emitter Control," said the *Argonaut's* science officer over the comm. "Initialize stabilization process."

"Initializing stabilization process Janeway Mark 36." *And may the 36th time be the charm!*

The soft chorus of chirps and beeps in the room

grew faster and faster as readouts shifted with increasing speed. "Data stream steady," reported Kathryn.

"Substations on-line and working," Pol added.

From the bridge the science officer suddenly said, "Emitter Control, geothermal levels are rising. Stations Two and Seven heading for critical!" Luminous red flowers bloomed on Kathryn's status display.

"Acknowledged," said Kathryn, her fingers dancing over the controls. "Shifting loads across Stations One, Five, Nine and Twelve." The flowers cooled back to green.

"Stations back within safety margins," Pol chimed in. "Geothermal is stable."

"Bridge, this is Engineering," came a new voice over the comm speaker. "Warp generators operating at one hundred ten percent of rated capacity. This level is sustainable for only a short time. Seconds would be better than minutes, sir."

"Acknowledged, Engineering," said the science officer. "Emitter control, status."

Immediately Pol reported, "Substations holding, core field readings within specs. Containment is now feasible."

Quietly pleased at the Diasoman's efficiency, Kathryn reported, "Containment field forming." She held her breath as a glowing ball surrounded Epsilon One's core on the schematic display. A sudden flood of data hit the console as all twelve planetary substations twisted the fabric of space itself to defy the resistance of gravity and mass to reshape the structure of a

planet. Kathryn's fingers danced across the control surfaces, persuading red lights to turn green.

But there were too many red lights and her fingers too few and too slow to stem the crimson tide.

Lights suddenly began cooling to green and Kathryn was dimly aware that a second pair of hands was dancing across her board. A rhythm developed between the four hands, crossing lightly over to tap out new red blooms. Twenty fingers danced an intricate improvised ballet of cooperation and control.

"Containment field established!" crowed Pol, as the last red light faded to green.

"Bridge, the core is contained. Estimated stabilization in"—Kathryn calculated swiftly—"forty seconds."

"This is going to be close, Bridge," warned Engineering.

Kathryn swallowed. *Please, don't make everything blow up again, please please please!* For forty infinitely long seconds she watched her console readouts so closely she forgot to even breathe. Her hands moved across the touchpads automatically now, keeping everything in her jurisdiction under control. Behind her she could hear Pol, back at her own console, booping and beeping as the Diasoman kept the rest of the job under control as well.

A light on Kathryn's instrument panel flashed. She inhaled with a gasp. "Bridge, the core containment bubble has reshaped the core fields. Reducing field strength. Stand by."

"Field strength reducing," Pol called out. A long

moment passed. "It looks like it's going to hold!" Pol shouted. "We did it!"

Kathryn exhaled deeply. "Bridge. Stabilization accomplished."

"Acknowledged, Emitter Control. Engineering, get those warp generators back down!"

"Cutting warp power, Bridge. Disengaging generators from emitter. We're clear."

"Emitter Control, status."

Giddy with success, Kathryn said, "Geothermal levels dropping to normal, sir."

"All substations on-line and maintaining new core configuration," added Pol.

Kathryn caught Pol's eye and grinned. "Bridge, Epsilon One is stable."

With a gentle shimmer the Emitter Control Room of the starship *Argonaut* disappeared, leaving Kathryn standing in the empty holosuite with Pol. "Congratulations," came the bland voice of the computer. "You have passed the test."

Kathryn wasn't sure which of them whooped the loudest, but both she and Pol let out a yell and hugged each other, hardly fitting behavior for Starfleet cadets. Kathryn didn't care. For once she just didn't care. "We did it!" she cried.

"We did it we did it we did it!" Pol repeated, clapping her furry hands in glee. "And see?" She lifted her arm. "I'm not twitching!"

Their battles won, Kathryn and Pol returned to Sudak Hall and reported to Mallet's office. Despite the late hour, Kathryn knew he'd still be there. As she suspected, he'd been monitoring their progress. "Congratulations, cadets," he said when they entered. He raised an eyebrow at Kathryn. "You see? There was a solution."

Kathryn blushed with embarrassment, but she remained standing at attention. Admitting a mistake and enduring the consequences was part of being a good Starfleet officer. "Yes, sir, there was. I suppose I didn't see that solution because I was looking for a fault in the scenario . . . not in myself."

"Not all tests are purely intellectual," said Mallet. "As for you, Cadet Pol, I'm pleased to see you beginning to handle your separation anxieties. You and your sister are making admirable progress."

Pol grinned. "Thank you, sir!"

"Now, the hour is late and I'm sure we're all tired after such a trying evening. That will be all, cadets. Dismissed!"

Pol left first. Just as Kathryn was about to follow her out, Mallet said, "Oh, and Cadet Janeway."

She turned. "Yes, sir?"

He picked up a program chip from his desk. "You know as well as I that you don't need this anymore. However, I shall *unofficially* hold it for you until graduation. Do you understand?"

"I think I do, sir," said Kathryn. "I think I do."

Chapter

11

Early the next morning, Kathryn headed for CGC Mallet's office as ordered. But just as she reached the Main Lounge on the first floor, she stopped dead at the sight of a Starfleet officer sitting on a couch near the CGC's door. The officer was a vice admiral. Specifically, the officer was Vice Admiral Edward Janeway. "Daddy!" Kathryn blurted in surprise.

Her father smiled and stood. "Hello, Goldenbird. I see you've managed to survive until I got here."

Kathryn's first impulse was to run into his arms, but she quickly checked herself. *You're a Starfleet cadet now,* she thought. *Daddy will want to see you act like one.* Keeping her pace at a steady walk but grinning like mad at the same time, Kathryn approached her father. "Hi, Daddy."

To her surprise, he drew her into a warm bear hug. "What is this? You're acting like an old retired admiral already," he commented dryly. "The Academy must be a lot stricter nowadays than when I was a cadet." He gestured at Kathryn's uniform. "You look good," he said with evident pride.

Kathryn beamed. "I still can't believe I'm really wearing this. Sometimes I do a doubletake when I see myself in the mirror."

"Wait until you start collecting pips." Vice Admiral Janeway gestured at the couch. "Sit down. Tell me what you've been up to."

They sat, but Kathryn didn't know where to begin. There was so much to tell her father, but she was still stunned at seeing him. First he hadn't come when she'd expected him, and now he was there when she didn't expect him. She didn't know if she should feel angry or happy or something in-between. *Take Amelia's advice,* she finally thought. *Don't be mad at him, just be proud of him.* "It hasn't been easy," she said, "but I think I'm settling in now." She told him about ThrumPol and her classes and the dorm drills, ending with, "CGC Mallet's really got his eye on me, though." She jerked a thumb at Mallet's closed office door. "When he goes back to his duties as the Chair of the Sciences Department, I have a feeling he's going to run me ragged."

"It'll be good for you," Janeway said, only half jokingly. "Let's face it, you haven't chosen an easy life path, Goldenbird, but you have chosen a fulfilling one. I'm glad to see you're handling it well."

The events of the past two weeks flashed like a speeded-up holopic through Kathryn's mind. *I'm handling it as best I can,* she thought. Then she noticed her father grow somber.

"Kathryn," he said slowly, "I owe you an apology. I promised to come with you on your first day at the Academy, but I didn't. I hope you understand that the Vulcan conference was no small matter. The meeting I had to attend after that was crucial as well."

Kathryn's throat felt as if a small planet were lodged there. She swallowed, willing her voice not to give out on her. "I understand, Daddy. It's okay."

"You sure?" He looked deep into her eyes. "I know how much that day meant to you."

Kathryn nodded, more sure now than ever. The look on his face at that moment was all the apology she could ever want. "Don't worry about it."

"Good. I'm glad you're not angry with me because that would spoil my plans."

"Plans?" Kathryn asked hopefully.

"That's right. I have three days on earth before I have to go to Alpha Centuri, and I intend to spend two of them here in San Francisco."

"Really?" Kathryn hugged her father tight. "Two whole days?"

"Well . . ." Janeway paused. "There are one or

two meetings I must attend at Starfleet Headquarters. But—"

Kathryn pulled back. "How many?"

"One tomorrow afternoon, and one"—he glanced at his wrist chrono—"oh, right about now."

As if on cue, CGC Mallet's door *whooshed* open and Mallet's head poked through. He looked at Kathryn. "Ah, Cadet Janeway, I see you and the vice admiral have found each other. Excellent." He turned to Kathryn's father. "Just a couple more minutes, Ed," he said, and disappeared back into his office again.

Kathryn's eyes bugged. "You two know each other! Commander Mallet told me to report first thing in the morning—he knew you were going to be here!"

Janeway was amused by his daughter's reaction. "Etienne and I served together years ago. Way too many years ago," he added, fingering the gray hairs at his temple. "He's an amazing man, Kathryn. You'll learn a lot from him."

"Believe me, I already have," Kathryn said earnestly. "But what are you two going to do right now?"

"Breakfast."

Despite her best efforts, Kathryn knew her expression registered disappointment.

Her father noticed. "Now don't worry, Goldenbird. I'll be back within an hour. If I didn't know him better, I'd suspect that Etienne just wanted to ask my advice on how to handle *you*."

Kathryn knew her father was kidding with her, but she still cringed a little with the thought that Mallet

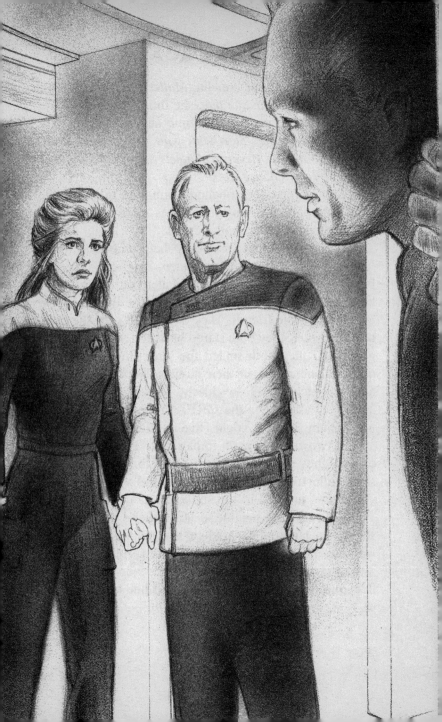

might tell him about Amelia. *Mallet is tough, but he'd never embarrass me like that,* she thought. Calming her anxiety, she decided it was time she started to trust other people more. *Start with your own father, Kathryn. After all, he never really let you down, did he? Give Mallet a chance, too.*

Mallet's office door opened again, and this time the CGC stepped out, his manners as crisp as his commander's uniform. "Shall we, Ed?"

Janeway stood up. "One hour," he promised Kathryn.

She just stared at the two men, maybe a little too boldly. Her first impression of Mallet had been right— he was the same height as her father. The two somehow even looked like friends. They both stood with the same proud posture, they both stared back at her with piercing gazes, and they both smiled the same smile—that little quirk at one corner of their mouths. No wonder Mallet always watched her so closely, and no wonder he'd known to assign her the GREASY test. He knew her better than she ever could have guessed.

The two officers grew impatient. "That will be all, cadet," they said, both at the same time and with the same inflection, almost like ThrumPol. "Dismissed!"

Kathryn jumped at the sound of their sharp voices. Then she saw the twinkle in her father's eyes and she started to laugh. That's when she caught sight of the wall chrono. "Oh my gosh, I'm late for class!"

Kathryn dashed away to face another day at Starfleet Academy, her spirits high and her future bright.

About the Authors

BOBBI JG WEISS and DAVID CODY WEISS are writing partners. They're also married. And they have lots of cats. Day after day they slog away at their computers, wracking their brains to write up fanciful and often absurd stories that they then sell to publishers. They have written a whole lot of stuff, among them novels *(Are You Afraid of the Dark?: The Tale of the Shimmering Shell; Star Trek: The Next Generation: Starfleet Academy: Breakaway;* and *The Secret World of Alex Mack: Close Encounters),* novel adaptations *(Sabrina, the Teenage Witch* and *Jingle All the Way),* comic books *(Pinky and the Brain, Animaniacs),* trading cards *(Batman and Robin, Star Trek Universe, James Bond Connoisseur Collection),* and other weird stuff like clothing tag blurbs, office catalog copy, and little squeezy books for kids who can't read yet so they just look at the pictures and squeeze the squeezy toy.

Bobbi and David hope to be filthy rich one day because laughing all the way to the bank sounds like fun.

Sometimes, it takes a kid to solve a good crime....

Original stories based on the hit Nickelodeon show!

#1 A Slash in the Night
by Alan Goodman
#2 Takeout Stakeout
By Diana G. Gallagher

#3 Hot Rock
by John Peel
(Coming in mid-August 1997)

#4 Rock 'n' Roll Robbery
by Lydia C. Marano and David Cody Weiss
(Coming in mid-October 1997)

To find out more about *The Mystery Files of Shelby Woo* or any other Nickelodeon show, visit Nickelodeon Online on America Online (Keyword: NICK) or send e-mail (NickMailDD@aol.com).

A MINSTREL® BOOK

Published by Pocket Books

1338-01